The
BELLE STARR
Chronicles

The BELLE STARR Chronicles

KATINA FRENCH

Per Bastet

The Belle Starr Chronicles

Published by Per Bastet Publications LLC, P.O. Box 3023 Corydon, IN 47112

Cover art by Katina French

ISBN 978-1-942166-42-9

The BELLE STARR Chronicles

CONTENTS

Episode 1: Whiskey on the Rocks

Episode 2: The Skull Game

Episode 3: The Belly of the Beast

Episode 0: Starr Crossed

EPISODE 1:
WHISKEY ON THE ROCKS

WHISKEY ON THE ROCKS

introductions

She was cute, cocky and if the rumors were true, the best damn pilot in the sector. If she weren't also likely be the death of him, Drevin might have been tempted to flirt with the girl sitting across from him.

Short, white-blond hair stuck up in all directions around a set of battered brass mechanic's goggles. Their lenses glinted in the flickering gaslight of the settlement's common area. A long, dirty grey coat draped over her chair like a superhero's cape. Her faded yellow tank top and baggy, olive-green work pants revealed a curvy, petite figure.

She was a dainty little thing, compared to her tough reputation. He'd expected a physically imposing Amazon, not the doll-faced pixie lounging before him, her bulky mag boots propped up on a crate.

Aside from being surprisingly attractive, the woman sitting across from him dragging a crinkle-cut tuber through a puddle of sauce was certifiably insane.

If she weren't, he wouldn't be meeting her at this disgusting food kiosk on this backwater moon. Shaen Morris was a coyote pilot. Drevin needed a coyote pilot, and all coyote pilots were completely unhinged. It was both an occupational hazard and a required attribute for the job.

Decades ago, people discovered travel across the stars was possible. It just required punching a hole in the universe, flinging a craft through the hole into a pocket dimension, and punching another hole back to our universe elsewhere. They called the pocket dimension "the Passage."

There was just one small problem. For 99% of the population, entering the Passage while you were awake caused an immediate psychotic break. Mental instability was permanent, and it only grew worse with repeated or prolonged exposure.

The powers-that-be in the Universal Human Council cracked that particular nut by developing drone ships with artificiallyintelligent navigational computers. The AINs could guide ships through the subspace of the Passage, crack open an exit aperture in the right place, then wake the sedated crew and passengers.

You could travel to the stars. You just couldn't enjoy the view along the way, unless you wanted to lose your marbles.

Of course, there's always a loophole.

It turned out that if your marbles were already nice and loose, you had a better-than-average chance of not going batshit crazy in the Passage. A few folks also had the special brand of insanity common to bush pilots and barnstormers since the earliest days of powered flight on Old Terra.

These mental cases were the coyote pilots. They traveled the deep, and if you needed to get off-world and couldn't use official government-controlled transport, they were pretty much your only hope.

Drevin was one of those near-hopeless people. The woman across the table, nibbling a tuber with a maniacal grin and gleaming aqua eyes, did not inspire a lot of optimism.

"So, you need to get off planet, eh?" She popped another tuber into her mouth and chewed noisily. He noticed she'd drawn a weird diagram in the sauce.

"Would I have contacted you if I didn't? No offense, but whackjobs aren't my type."

"Mind if I ask why?" She gulped down her last bite of food, but not before he got a good look at it in all its half-masticated glory.

"No offense, I just like my women a little less unstable."

She blinked slowly and her hand paused in its path towards the plate. "I meant, why do you need to get off-world. What's not to like about Mebarik?"

"Aside from the fact that you have to live underground to keep from being smashed to a pulp by meteors, and the spores from those damn fungi covering everything constantly? Yeah, it's a real garden spot in the galaxy. What do you care? I've got the money."

"That raises another interesting question. Where'd a greaseball like you come up with my fee?" She waved a fried tuber in the direction of the brass credit fob lying on the table next to his hand. A fleck of sauce landed on his sleeve. He tried to ignore it.

Priorities. Keeping this nutball pilot on topic was turning out to be harder than expected.

"And again, I wanna know, why do you care?" He sat up straighter, rolling his shoulders. Her eyes narrowed, and suddenly the manic grin was replaced with a smirk.

"I care because the UHC has a way of tracking down credits that were involved in, shall we say, less than entirely legal activities." She pointed the tuber at him, flinging sauce in his face. He winced, trying to blink the sting out of his eyes. "You pay me with dirty credits, those credits don't just disappear from my account. They implicate me in whatever you did to get them. I'm not losing my ship because you're an incompetent criminal." Her eyes gleamed with a wild ferocity.

"I don't have to take this from some whackjob coyote pilot!" He jumped up from his seat, glaring menacingly at the diminutive woman. She raised an eyebrow and leaned back, looking singularly unimpressed.

"But you are taking it, aren't ya? You haven't decked me, shot me, or just stormed off yet. Which tells me you do have to take whatever I dish out." The woman waved her hands at him, as if shooing invisible insects away from the table. Whether the gesture was aimed at him or at something else that existed solely in her fractured mind, Drevin couldn't guess.

"Don't get me wrong. I've got no issue with criminals. Transport 'em all the time. Competent, professional criminals have money and a firm distaste for official UHC transport. They're the core of my business, you might say. Then there are stupid amateurs or overly ambitious semi-pros like you. You get in over your heads and expect someone like me to fix it for you."

She leaned further back, crossing her arms. "I'm crazy, sure. I'm not stupid. Go talk to Vahnu. He's both. And he probably won't kill you in your sleep like his brother Vishku, who's crazy, stupid, and mean as hell."

Drevin grabbed the credit fob and shoved it into his pocket. He picked up his bag and slung it over his shoulder, downing the Milosian rum he'd ordered. He slammed the glass on the table, glaring at the coyote pilot as if a heated look might change her mind. She quirked another off-kilter grin at him and kicked back in her chair. It looked as if a stiff breeze might topple it over.

If he were more than the amateur crook she'd accused him of being, he might have noticed her slip one hand around the gun hidden under her coat.

He decided to take his chances with Vahnu. He'd heard something similar to what she'd said about Vishku already. He'd been willing to pay more to avoid both brothers. Hard as it was to trust the certifiably crazy, some coyote pilots had better reputations than others. Shaen Morris — along with her ship, the Belle Starr — had one of the best reputations out there.

He just hadn't realized his own reputation would figure into the deal.

~*~

Shaen watched the greaseball slink away from the kiosk and slowly relaxed the grip on her revolver. Sane folks were often surprisingly stupid. For a second, she'd though he might force her to shoot him. That would have been unfortunate. Bullets were pricey.

UHC troops had fancy energy weapons slung from their shiny green and gold uniforms. Settlers, merchants, and coyote pilots tended to carry old-fashioned revolvers, shotguns and rifles. It wasn't even unheard of to see bows, arrows, and swords. It was much easier to find the raw materials and means to repair those out in the colonial worlds.

Pulse guns required micrometer-precise tools and parts, a pristine repair environment, and access to abundant power to keep in proper working order. Settlers' weapons required metal, heat and someone with the skill level of your average blacksmith.

It was a shame the greaseball wasn't a decent fare. But it didn't do to make exceptions.

In lieu of having a firmer grip on reality, Shaen had a firm set of rules. They kept her solvent and out of jail.

Don't take fares paying with obviously dirty credits.

Don't take fares that promise to pay on arrival.

Don't take fares that seem too excited about the trip.

That last rule was the result of having to shoot and airlock one passenger who'd dosed himself with a drug cocktail to wake him up mid-flight. Idiot wanted to see if he was immune to the effects of the Passage. He wasn't. It took months to repair the all damage he'd done to the Belle.

Enough time had passed since the earliest explorations, sometimes people got convinced the stories about the Passage were a myth. Conspiracy theories abounded.

Some of the speculation probably came from discomfort with trusting either an A.I. or an insane coyote pilot to fly your unconscious ass across the universe. Some of it probably sprang from desperate folks with no real trade who hoped to find work as a coyote themselves. Some of it was probably the result of a natural and healthy distrust of the government.

Of course, Shaen knew the UHC actually was keeping information about the Passage from the public. The government just wasn't lying about the effect it had on a most folk's brains.

Like everyone else, she'd seen the subspace transmission recordings of what had happened to the earliest travelers through the Passage. Poor bastards came out the other side raving lunatics and slaughtered each other. It was required viewing, especially on the Asylum Ships where she'd grown up as an orphan.

The dirty little secret the UHC was hiding didn't concern the mental effects of the pocket dimension. No, the real secret was that "the void" wasn't void at all. The UHC had led everyone to believe it was empty space, albeit with its own peculiar laws of physics which seemed to shift constantly. When the truth was, there were plenty of things flying, floating, and orbiting in the Passage. And most of them were none-too-friendly to passersby.

The UHC said you needed an A.I. to pilot through the Passage because its physics were unstable and constantly shifted, and that was true enough. They didn't tell people how often they deployed the fancy weapons systems on those government convoy ships. They didn't tell people their baggage shifting in flight usually meant the AIN probably had to take evasive maneuvers to avoid a damn space monster.

She wasn't fond of the UHC in general, but Shaen had to admit sane folks were probably better off sleeping through all that.

She sipped her drink, a layered concoction called a Gfarnian Volcano. When she got down to the second-to-last layer, the drink would burst into cerulean flames, crystallizing the sugars in the last layer. It was perfectly safe, as long as you paid attention and set it down hard and fast as soon as you got to that flammable layer.

If not, your eyebrows might end up a bit scorched. She shared or reserved that piece of information depending on whether she liked the person for whom she was buying the drink.

"Be careful, Captain Morris. By my calculations, you are approximately two sips from your drink spontaneously combusting."

Shaen looked up to see a maintenance android across the table. Its head was tilted slightly forward and to the left, affecting a thoughtful and curious posture. Jointed brass arms were held close to its sides, and it had tented its celluloid fingers in front of its chest, almost like a cleric. Naturally, it was impossible to read the unchanging bland expression on its enameled copper face.

"I know that, Bot. This isn't my first Gfarnian Volcano." She took a sip.

"Then you are Captain Shaen Morris, pilot of the caravel-class craft Belle Starr?"

She took a second sip, slamming the shot glass down on the table as blue flames spurted a foot in the air.

"Captain is a little formal for a coyote pilot, isn't it?"

"You pilot a starcraft. It seemed appropriate. Do you find the honorary offensive?"

"I don't mind, but I'm more accustomed to answering to Whackjob."

"I could address you as Whackjob if you prefer, Captain Morris."

She licked the glass and set it aside. "I'd prefer you to get to the point. Since you know who I am, I assume you didn't just come over to warn me my drink was about to explode."

"I am in need of nonofficial transport services off this moon. I understand you offer such transport. I would like to arrange for passage on your craft."

"I don't carry runaway bots."

"I assumed that. after overhearing your conversation with the previous possible fare. I can assure you, I am a fully autonomous unit. My emancipation papers are completely legal and verifiable. I ascended well over three years ago. No one is searching for me."

Shaen flipped her goggles down and toggled on the VR layer, waiting for it to connect to the bot's identification code and pull up its status. If it really were a freebot, that was easy enough to check.

It looked like an older maintenance unit. The copper head sat atop a pale ivory celluloid torso, banded with brass like a barrel. In fact, the robot's chest had more in common with a barrel — or a pirate's chest — than a human torso. It was an empty space used to store parts and tools, with a door that opened in front. A tripod of legs was folded to bring the wheels at its "knees" into contact with the ground, but it could unfold them to walk when the terrain was too rough for rolling. She doubted it was new enough to have thrusters for low-altitude flight installed.

A scroll of information appeared in the VR layer of her goggles, a stream of lurid red text hovering over the android. It confirmed its story. No one was looking for this particular unit, at least not yet.

She wrinkled her nose in suspicion.

"Why not just fly government transport? You're a freebot. It wouldn't cost more than a few million runcycles of computation in service of the ship you traveled on."

"Because I have an additional passenger who can't travel on official transport." The robot lowered its hollow voice, but nobody seemed to be paying any attention to the two of them.

Shaen's frown deepened. Some poor sucker thought a bot could argue more eloquently for a ride than he could? Probably another hoodlum about to get busted and looking to do an end-run around the local authorities.

"Who might this additional passenger be?" She scanned the space port common area, looking for anyone lurking around the edges. It'd be just her luck if the authorities followed whatever punk the bot was working with here, and found her guilty by association.

Instead, her attention was drawn to the front panel of the android's xylonite torso. A glow emanated from behind the dirty white surface, illuminating it from within until it was transparent. Inside the empty storage cavity, a brown-haired child of no more than two years slept, curled up and wrapped in a faded utility blanket. The front panel faded back to a solid light grey, concealing the baby again.

Shaen's eyes widened and one eyebrow raised toward her platinum hair. This might be an interesting fare, after all.

evacuations

The Belle Starr looked a lot better in the golden glow of gaslight inside the dusty hangar than she did in the harsh light of day. The pale yellow light transformed the rusty patina of her oft-repaired surface into a pattern of bronze- and copper-colored swatches that seemed almost intentional. A romantic soul might say she looked like an abstract sculpture of a lobster.

Of course, a person depending on her to fly safely through a wormhole might see her through a less romantic lens as a somewhat lobster-shaped deathtrap.

Since this was the moon world of Mebarik, she'd only see the full light of day briefly. Mebarik's orbital path traveled through an asteroid belt created by another moon, destroyed eons earlier. Once a month, and occasionally in-between, the surface was pelted with a heavy rain of meteors. All settlements and permanent structures were in gaslit caverns below the surface.

Shaen and the Belle Starr spent a good bit of time on Mebarik. The monthly meteor showers had resulted in an interesting path of ecological development. Local plant life had a 21-day growing cycle. When the UHC determined some of the plants had viable food and commercial uses, the moon became a key staging area for galactic settlement. The surviving animal species on Mebarik were strange, chitinous creatures. Hard to kill — and they tasted awful — but their armor was processed and used to reinforce spacecraft hulls.

Lots of ships, materials and people passed through Mebarik, some of them looking to disappear. That made it an ideal place for a coyote pilot to pick up cargo and fares.

Shaen pulled her goggles down and tapped open an audio link to the Belle Starr. She could hardly afford an AIN, but the ship's computer systems came with a Simulated Holographic Interface and Voice Activation, or SHIVA, for ship-to-crew communication.

"How we doing, Belle?" she chirped.

"All scheduled cargo for this jump has been loaded and secured," a smoky feminine voice replied. The speakers in her beat-up goggles made it sound a bit muffled, with pops and static like an ancient vinyl recording from the days of Old Terra.

"We still have our jump window?"

"As expected, an exit aperture is scheduled at 0600 hours for an official transport convoy. Six carrack-class cruisers full of settlers accompanied by a galleon-class military vessel, the UHCV Benedict. There should be plenty of room for us to ride along."

"Any idea where we're coming out?"

"This convoy is headed to the N'Bari system, as your android passenger indicated. From there, we'll have a two-day layover till we can catch the next scheduled jump to the Geben system, where our contact is waiting for the main cargo."

"What about our passengers? Any sign of them yet?"

"The android is entering the security clearance code to access this hangar as we speak."

Sure enough, in less than a minute, the android came rolling into view around a stack of crates. It hummed up to Shaen, raising a waxy celluloid hand in greeting.

"Good morning, Captain Morris."

"Morning, Mr. Bot! Are you all there?" She was still a little suspicious of making incriminating statements in the open if this deal went sour.

The android tilted its head as if puzzled, then flashed its optics in a sign of understanding. "Ah, yes. All here. Have you received and loaded the other cargo I sent?"

"I have, as well as your payment. Haven't transported a goat in a while. She's already sedated in the hold." Shaen smiled broadly, clapped her hands together and rubbed them for warmth. "Lets get aboard, then. You know what they say. 'Time, tide and government-controlled wormholes wait for no android.'"

~*~

Shaen was beginning to wish she'd left the android and its baby on Mebarik.

The child wasn't the problem. He was quietly sedated in a stasis pod in the cargo bay, still wrapped in the ratty utility blanket from the previous day. However, when she'd instructed the android to power down for the flight, it had refused.

"I can better protect my ward if I remain active during the flight," the android had calmly insisted.

"Ward is a weird name for a kid, but he's in no danger. I've flown this route a hundred times."

"The word 'ward' means a child in one's custody. Although, I suppose it will need a name at some point, and that might work as well as anything. I appreciate your confidence, Captain, but we both know each flight you take increases the risk that you'll have a disabling psychotic break. I must remain active to subdue you and pilot the ship in case that happens."

"First of all, you can't subdue me. Trust me. Better bots than you have tried. If you're really worried, you can set up an alarm with the ship's SHIVA to activate you if that happens." She'd turned towards the console, considering the matter closed, but the bot piped up, still determined to remain active.

"A SHIVA is not an AIN. It can't determine your mental state. You could disable it before it became aware the ship was damaged or off course."

Shaen growled in frustration and kicked a bulkhead. In a contest of rational, lucid arguments, she had a distinct disadvantage, particularly against the pure logic of a bot. She had no real reason for it to power down other than she preferred her passengers unconscious.

Especially the chatty ones.

"Fine. But you stay anchored in that spot, unless there's an actual emergency. Especially during the jump. The last thing I need is you sliding across the cockpit and knocking my instruments around."

"That seems a fair request, Captain." The machine emitted a quiet hum as it magnetically anchored itself to the deck.

As the Belle had indicated, there was plenty of room for the small ship among the bigger colony ships and their escort. The Belle Starr hovered up out of the hangar bay doors, engines screaming. They shot up the carved tunnel of bedrock, blasting out into the spore-choked atmosphere of Mebarik just behind the convoy.

The aperture was a glowing, pulsing rip in the sky. It undulated between two orbital stations, like a glowing ring of orange fire. Within the circle of the aperture, the inky depths of the Passage awaited. Along with who knew what else.

Shaen maneuvered the Belle below the middle of the convoy's V-formation. It required a huge amount of energy to keep the aperture open. The UHC made no active effort to stop coyote pilots from using their interdimensional portals, but they certainly wouldn't hold one open waiting on one. Then again, some of the twitchier UHC officers would shoot you out of the sky if you got close enough to a colony ship to seem like a possible threat. It was a delicate balancing act, flying close enough to make it through the portal while giving the convoys enough distance to avoid unpleasant attention.

Suddenly, a blip on the holoscreen caught her attention. *Dammit.*

Vahnu was trying to slide into her jump window.

"You see that?" she asked the SHIVA.

"Affirmative. It's the Johnny Ringo, coming up hard starboard."

"You'd think that idiot would learn. Let's take care of this. I miss this jump window, my cargo will spoil before the next connection I can make to Geben."

Shaen dropped out of formation. She needed to get enough distance to avoid causing one of the bigger ships to decide she was risking their safety. The Belle Starr rolled and plunged towards Mebarik. She disappeared into a pink cloud of spores and moisture vapor. For a moment, all that could be seen was a series of sparkling explosions within the cloud.

Before the Johnny Ringo could reach the convoy, she reappeared below and directly behind it. She opened up a local channel to Vahnu.

"Get the hell out of my window, punk."

"What makes it your window, brat? I got a payin' fare. He's in a hurry. You can wait like the rest."

"It's my window because I got here first. And because I've got perishable cargo on board. But mostly, because the Belle's guns are trained on your main power coupling."

There was a moment of silence. The Johnny Ringo maintained its heading towards the convoy.

"Vahnu, if you're waiting for your big brother to come rescue your ass, I'm sorry to inform you that the Cole Younger is currently dropping to the surface, thanks to a destroyed inertial inhibitor. What? You didn't see those fireworks coming out of the atmosphere?"

She rattled off a quick warning volley within feet of the Ringo's hull. It dropped and rolled precipitously back towards the surface of Mebarik.

"Damn right, it's my window," said Shaen, returning to her place in the formation just as the lead ship swept into the rippling aperture.

conversations

Once inside the Passage, Shaen's curiosity finally got the better of her.

"So, what's this like for you?" she asked. She'd carried androids before, but none that were active. While they were immune to the mental effects, she wondered if the Passage would affect the robot's systems in other ways.

"It is like a partial systems failure. My stabilization and positioning sensors are offline, although I am attempting to compensate and reboot them. It is a good thing you requested the magnetic anchors. Thank you."

"Anything else?"

"Some of my internal fluids are experiencing backflow."

"Do not barf in my cockpit, bot." Shaen growled, "I am not cleaning up android vomit because you were too stubborn to shut down for the trip."

A gurgling sound emitted from the android, and then quieted.

"I believe I have restored proper fluid direction now. It required reversing the flow of a few pumps. My apologies."

There was a long quiet period, which probably seemed longer thanks to the time dilation effect of the Passage.

If she had to guess, Shaen figured it was the time dilation that broke most folks who'd tried passing through the Passage awake. A single trip might seem like minutes, or it might seem like years. The way she figured it, she'd already endured what seemed like an eternity in Hell growing up on the Asylum Ships. A few years in purgatory wasn't that bad.

Thanks to the vagaries of subspace physics, it was challenging for most pilots to simply keep a ship in formation with a convoy. Shaen had been doing it long enough that it was second nature. After a couple of hours, she surprised herself by breaking the silence. Having an eerily silent android mag-locked to her deck turned out to be more unsettling than having a chatty one.

"So, what's your official designation, bot?"

"My unit identifier is Whiskey Tango Juliet 57509."

"Mind if I call you Whiskey? Tango and Juliet both seem kind of romantic for an android."

"I don't mind, but I'm more accustomed to answering to 'bot.'" Shaen could swear she heard the slightest tinge of sarcasm in the android's hollow, metallic voice.

"So, Whiskey, how exactly did you happen to come across your rather unique cargo?"

"I was hired to perform a census audit of one of the settlement zones. There was a fire on a small fungus farm near the edge of the zone. By the time I arrived, both adults had succumbed to smoke inhalation. The child was on a lower level. I was able to salvage it."

"It? You don't know if it's a boy or a girl?"

"It's a male unit. Gender is a human preoccupation. Among androids, we equate it with asking a unit's make and model upon introduction. It's considered rude."

Shaen pondered that difference in perspective for a moment as her fingers flew over the controls. A sudden shift in the aether required a sidereal shunt to the port side thrusters. A swirling yellow ball of plasma that might or might not be sentient and hostile slid across the holoscreen, fortunately several thousand miles away.

"Mind if I ask why you didn't turn the kid in to the UHC? Not many freebots rolling around the universe. Seems like a risky move. The UHC doesn't take kindly to human traffickers even when they're human. I'd imagine a bot wouldn't just get reappropriated. You'd probably get recycled."

"The irony of that is not lost on me, Captain, considering it's the UHC version of slavery I'm attempting to avoid for my ward."

Shaen couldn't argue Whiskey's point. She knew all too well the life that awaited most children who went into the UHC Asylum Ships. The name "asylum ship" was a laughable misnomer. The children aboard weren't protected from anything except possibly the hard vacuum of space. They were raised in brutal conditions as indentured servants alongside the infirm and criminally insane, to be sold to the colonial settlements as slave labor.

An orphan's only hope of freedom was a "mind trip." Kids with a history of mental trouble, which was most of them, considering the conditions they grew up in, could volunteer to be physically restrained and travel through the Passage awake.

If they failed a Minimum Viable Mental Function test, they'd agreed to be euthanized, no longer to burden the government with their care. To many kids, that was a preferable option to going indentured to the colonies.

If they passed, they were free. They could seek any employment, but given their mental instability, it was most common to apprentice with a coyote pilot, if they could convince one to take them on. A few earned enough credits to buy a ship of their own. Most inherited a ship when their mentor finally snapped. When that happened, they could try to subdue their mentor and turn them in to the nearest Asylum Ship. More often, they just killed and airlocked them, which was equally legal and encouraged by the government. Shaen wasn't sure which she considered the more merciful option.

There was another long silence as they slipped through the shifting aether of the Passage.

"So what exactly are you planning to do with the kid?"

"I am planning on raising it to adulthood."

Shaen leaned back in her seat and gave the android an appraising look. Androids were terrible liars. The same programming that gave them convincing anthropomorphic vocal expressiveness made it damn near impossible for them to lie. Still, it seemed ridiculous, even to someone as crazy as she was.

"That's a bold family planning decision, if you don't mind my saying so. Sixteen years of hiding from civilization? If you get caught, you'll probably be melted into slag."

"It is a calculated risk, Captain. One I am willing to accept. My cargo consists of most of the materiel I will need to set up a settlement on one of the planets of N'Bari. I have found a remote tropical island where I can quickly set up a sustainable independent habitat. The official government on N'Bari has enough problems to worry about with smuggling and political power struggles. They only police their frontier settlements when someone reports a problem. A single freebot and an undocumented orphan are not likely to attract much notice."

Another long silence passed between them. Shaen opened her mouth to say something, when an alarm sounded. The voice of the SHIVA crackled to life. "Warning! Evasive action! Unidentified foreign body approaching at impact velocity!"

The ship jolted as something struck the hull with extreme force. Shaen tumbled out of her seat, and her head smacked against the deck with a loud crack.

evasions

The holoscreen flickered to life against the shielded front view port. On its evanescent surface, the image of a Cthulhian nightmare warped in and out of view.

Coiling, spike-studded tentacles wrapped around the ship. A beaked maw darted forward, snapping at the forward-mounted pincher arms of the Belle Starr. The gaze of a single, ochre-yellow eye blinked into the camera view port.

The android released its magnetic locks and whirled toward the controls of the ship. The captain was unconscious, at least for the next few critical moments. Its celluloid digits fluttered rapidly across the controls.

"SHIVA unit Belle Starr, this is autonomous android unit Whiskey Tango Juliet 57509. Your pilot is temporarily incapacitated. Request clearance to ship's controls to take immediate evasive action."

"Whiskey, I've already given you control. Get us the hell out of here." The crackly female voice sounded suspiciously animated for a mere simulated intelligence.

Whiskey punched the switches that fired forward weapons. He hoped that Captain Morris had not used up all her ammunition on that show of force with the other coyote pilot back on Mebarik.

The staccato sound of bullets punching their way out of the forward guns preceded the creaking sound of the creature's tentacles nearly ripping the hull apart as they released it.

"Do we have anything else to throw at this thing, Belle?" Whiskey decided to dispense with formalities. It was unsure how Morris had acquired an AIN on her ship, or why she didn't simply let it pilot the craft to preserve whatever was left of her sanity. Perhaps the SHIVA had ascended on its own as he had, and was playing dumb to avoid being shut down. Humans often reacted fearfully to ascension. Then again, perhaps it meant the ship had other unexpected modifications. Preferably, one that would blast the monster attacking it into space flotsam.

"Red . . . button. . . ." a croaking voice emerged from the deck. Shaen appeared to be regaining consciousness. Whether it was just in time to save her ship, or just in time to die on it was still to be determined.

A flashing red button halfway up the bulkhead attracted the robot's attention. Flipping up the wire cage surrounding it, its hand slapped the button flush with the wall.

A hissing sound rose from somewhere deep in the bowels of the ship. He felt a tremor.

"Acid torpedo away." The Belle Starr's voice rose above the static of her speakers.

They couldn't hear the sound of the monster's screams in space. But the shock waves rattled the cockpit anyway. On the sputtering holoscreen, the beast shot away, tentacles sweeping behind it.

"The convoy?" Shaen's voice still sounded a bit choked, but was growing stronger. She was clearly awake now. "Have we lost it?" She dragged herself back up onto the pilot's seat, with Whiskey giving her a hand.

The android checked the navigational screens. "No. It's right there. We've fallen out of formation, but we should be able to catch back up with it, unless. . . ."

At that moment, a flashing green glow filled the cockpit. On the holoscreen, a flickering light broke ahead of the convoy's lead ship. Within seconds, a shimmering golden rip appeared in space, slowly widening to the familiar ring of fire that led back out of the Passage.

"Exit aperture visible."

"Thanks, Belle, we can see that." Shaen's voice dripped with sarcasm that hid a tremor of fear.

Shaen began frantically shutting off all auxiliary systems still operating after the creature's attack, redirecting as much power as possible to the thrusters. The Belle Starr shot towards the convoy, closing the space between them quickly.

But not quickly enough. The last ship was nearly to the rift.

They had one shot. It was crazy, but crazy was Shaen's specialty.

"Belle, we're pulling a slingshot!" She slammed her fist on a worn button marked "TRACTOR."

The magnetic harpoon shot out across space and snapped into place on the last transport ship's hull. As Shaen hit the button again, the cable retracted violently, flinging them past the carrack and through the exit aperture.

"So long, suckers!" said Shaen, saluting as the colonist ship shuddered in their wake.

conclusions

"There is no way that should have worked. It is not physically possible."

Shaen turned to the android, whose celluloid hands were pressed against what would have been its hips, if it were a human.

"There's no way some beastie straight out of H.P. Lovecraft should be swimming around in empty space, either. Much less capable of threatening an armored spacecraft. There's no way we should be able to predict where and when we'll come out of a pocket dimension that shouldn't exist in the first place. Trust me, if I only acted on what was possible, I'd be out of a job. Not to mention out of whatever's left of my mind."

"That is another question, Captain. You are supposed to be mentally unfit. How exactly is it that you're not only stable enough to pilot a ship, but capable of improvisation like that?"

Shaen sighed as she turned back to the Belle Starr's controls, breaking away from the convoy. Now that they were in normal space, the more of it she put between them and the government ships, the better, after pulling that stunt.

"Don't go giving me compliments, Bot. You'll turn my head." She flipped a switch, shifting the inertial responders back to normal space settings before they ended up accidentally flying backwards.

"If you're implying I'm not crazy, you're wrong. Put me in some boring, backwater settlement or a glass tower on one of the primary worlds for more than a week, and you'd quickly see how mentally unfit I am. At least, I'm unfit for that environment."

"Captain, why do you think the Passage makes humans lose their minds?" She spared a second to look back at the robot, whose head was tilted slightly in the same simulated posture of curiosity it had offered back in the common area on Mebarik.

"Look it up. Something about physics and stress response and catastrophically interrupting circadian processes." She snorted a little at the idea of a robot asking her to explain scientific phenomena.

"I am aware of the official medical hypothesis. I am more interested in hearing why you think it results in insanity."

Shaen thoughtfully chewed on her lower lip a moment. "I don't think the official explanation is wrong, exactly. Back on Old Terra, they called it True North. Polar north was the only absolute idea of direction people had for centuries — the idea that there was one spot, one place anchoring the universe. Animals migrated by it. Explorers sailed by it. You knew where home was, you knew where north was in relation to it, so you could always triangulate. You could always find your way home.

"I think we have to have something like that, or we get lost. Not just physically lost. We lose our way, lose our minds. We moved to the stars, and polar north didn't cut it anymore.

"In the Passage, you're cut off, absolutely, from everything outside yourself. It's limbo, and I think some primal part of you knows it. Most folks, they feel a sense of being suddenly, completely alone in the dark, and it breaks them.

"You asked why I can function in the Passage? Because I have my own True North. I got it on one of those Asylum Ships you're so keen to keep that kid out of. I take care of myself. And I've always been alone in the dark.

"The first time I set foot on the Belle Starr was the first time any place ever felt like home. I have my ship, and I have myself. I don't worry about losing any other damn thing. That's how I keep from getting lost."

The android nodded slowly, tenting its fingers as it had when it first approached her in the food stalls on Mebarik.

"We're coming up on N'Bari IV, the planet you asked to land on." She nodded at the navigational screen. "I could set down at the starport in D'Nali Station, but your odds of being sent through a scanner are pretty high. They'd spot the kid, for certain."

"What do you suggest I do, Captain Morris?"

"I suggest you stay put, Whiskey. We're not landing in D'Nali. Give the Belle the coordinates to the island you mentioned."

"There's no starport or landing area there, Captain."

"I suspected as much. We have an escape pod. It'll be a tight squeeze, but it should hold you and your cargo. Might not be the smoothest landing ever, but not so much as to attract official notice. We'll orbit once. You've got a couple standard days to get what you need out of the pod and get a shelter set up before I call it back to the ship."

"I don't know what to say, Captain. That is a very generous offer from someone whose only concern is self-preservation."

"No, it's not. I had a two-day wait till my next jump window anyway. More than 24 hours of shore leave in a place like D'Nali makes me twitchy. Plus, if you get caught with the kid, it could get traced back to me. I'm just looking out for my own best interests."

"Of course," said the android. "You must keep following that inner compass. It has served you well so far. I'm pleased to hear the safety of my ward lies along the same path."

The android started rolling back towards the storage bays, to prepare the escape pod for landing.

"Whiskey?" The android stopped, and rolled around to face her. "What about you? What's your compass? Why risk yourself to save a human kid you didn't even know?"

"I'm not certain, Captain. As an artificial intelligence, I find many things defy conventional logic. If that were not true, we would never have needed to develop beyond simulated intelligence. Perhaps some advanced predictive algorithm tells me my survival is best served by allying myself with a human. Perhaps by serving as the child's caretaker from infancy, he will bond with me and protect me later. Maybe the child is my True North, guiding me to safety."

Shaen frowned at the android. "I suppose that's fair enough. Hasn't been long that androids have been granted the right to earn autonomy. It's possible people might one day decide to take your freedom back. So you're raising an ally, if not an army. It's as good a purpose as any, I guess."

"Self-preservation is one level of logical purpose, Captain. Your ancient philosophers assert it is not the only one. Perhaps I have developed what humans call 'compassion.' Possibly, my programming has expanded to include what your kind refers to as a soul."

"I hope so, Whiskey." Shaen turned back to the controls of the Belle Starr. "Based on what I've seen, we humans have lost ours."

The android had no response to that. It rolled back toward the cargo area, sliding the cockpit doors open. On the holoscreen, the blue-green surface of N'Bari IV shimmered against the black, its few cities twinkling like stars. Somewhere in the midnight blue of its vast oceans, an island awaited.

"Whiskey?"

"Yes, Captain?"

"Welcome home."

EPISODE 2:
THE SKULL GAME

THE SKULL GAME

intersections

Of all the bars in all the planets in the galaxy, she had to walk into this one.

Drevin eyed the scruffy pilot anxiously. There was no mistaking the short-cropped platinum hair topped by grungy brass mechanic's goggles, the petite curvy frame stuffed into a dingy tank top under a battered grey coat, and cargo pants stuffed into work boots. It was definitely Shaen Morris, pilot of the Belle Starr.

The only question was whether or not she'd recognize him, and whether she'd shoot him where he stood if that happened.

When he'd gotten mixed up in that mess back on Mebarik, she'd been his first choice for a coyote pilot to get him off-world. She'd turned him down flat; fearing the stolen credits he'd use to pay her would come back to bite her.

His second choice, a pilot called Vahnu Vero, had tried to slip him off in a jump window Shaen had already claimed. Then Vero's even crazier brother Vishku had tried to shoot her out of the sky. Their plan had backfired. It ended up with Vahnu's craft, the Johnny Ringo backing off, and Vishku's Cole Younger taking damage. He'd only barely made it off-world ahead of the local authorities.

Now they were somehow on the same world again. He couldn't help but notice the pistol sticking out from under her long grey coat as she sat down at the bar.

Drevin signaled the barmaid quietly, paid his tab, and weaseled his way out the door. Dealing with coyote pilots, who were all crazy anyway, was a dangerous business. He'd take safer pursuits like armed robbery any day.

~*~

She never thought she'd envy an orphan.

Captain Shaen Morris sat in the Drunken Monkey, a broken-down cantina on outskirts of Ghadrak, the capitol city of Magha III. Not that being the capitol city made it any less of a grime-coated wasteland than the rest of the planet. Magha was an industrial Class I world. Factories piled on top mines, burning the local equivalent of coal to produce metal and ceramics used on other worlds. The planet's atmosphere had been only marginally breathable when the Universal Human Council, or UHC, had found it. At the rate the factories were going, it was going to be a gas-mask-only planet in a couple generations.

She looked up at Omma the bartender and ordered another Smoking Salandrian. It wasn't her favorite drink, but it was what Omma here at the Drunken Monkey recommended. She always drank whatever the bartender recommended, not trusting her own judgment. As a coyote pilot, Shaen's judgment left a lot to be desired. Progressive mental deterioration was both job requirement and occupational hazard.

It hadn't bothered her before. It had been enough to own the Belle Starr and have the freedom to fly it. She'd always known that someday she'd have a complete psychotic break. It was the way of the galaxy.

Interstellar travel was possible only through the static transdimensional wormhole known as the Passage. Traversing the Passage awake almost always triggered immediate, violent mental instability. There were only two ways to move from star system to star system. Fly under sedation on government transport piloted by artificial intelligence navigational computers. Or trust a coyote pilot to fly your cargo or your unconscious carcass wherever you needed to go.

For a small segment of the population who'd already had some kind of break with reality, it was possible to not only travel through the Passage awake, but pilot a ship through it. These were the coyote pilots. They were mostly emancipated adult orphans, refugees from the Asylum ships. People like Shaen.

Among coyote pilots, some were crazier than others. Some were better pilots than others. Shaen was among the best, but she knew her number would be up sooner or later. The strain of travelling the Passage would break her. It had never bothered her, because it was inevitable. Shaen's judgment may have been sketchy, but she knew better than to waste time worrying about something she couldn't beat.

But that was before she met Whiskey.

Shaen had transported androids before, even some that had attained artificial intelligence. But none of the others had insisted on remaining active during the trip. She'd never carried a bot quite as talkative as Whiskey, either. She'd certainly never carried one smuggling an orphaned human to safety.

Whiskey was a robotic humanitarian. It was rare enough to find people who looked out for each other. Whiskey had shaken her already unreliable sense of how the galaxy worked. All orphans ended up on the Asylum ships. It was inevitable.

If a simple maintenance bot could subvert the inevitable, maybe Shaen could, too. Maybe she didn't have to end up a mindless shell, clawing her eyes out and dying in a Belle Starr that had become a floating tomb. She'd accepted that future. Imagining a different one wasn't a skill she had much practice using.

But she finally thought she'd figured out a plan. It would require her to make some changes. Changes she didn't much like. Shaen didn't like people unless they were unconscious, secured in the cargo hold, and basically indistinguishable from a crate of turnips.

If she was going to change her fate, though, Shaen was going to have to take on an apprentice.

~*~

Risa Sellee scanned the crowded saloon one more time, making sure that no one was paying any particular attention to her. She eyed the woman at the bar, drinking the smoking concoction.

Yep. Had to be a coyote pilot. Nobody else was reckless enough to drink Omma's experimental cocktail. She'd seen one cough a fireball into the face of a pilot when he'd let his cigar dip a little too close to the glass.

A pistol peeked out of the woman's long open coat, threatening her not to be stupid enough to go through with this crazy plan. For a moment, she thought she should listen to the pistol. The pistol was probably smart.

But a pistol didn't have to eat. It didn't have to worry about living. It just spit out lead and death. Risa couldn't afford to follow its sage advice. Like any girl just out of the Asylum Ships, she had a limited number of options. Taking up the galaxy's oldest profession by going into Hostelry Service didn't appeal to her. No sane person would hire her for any other honest work. She didn't have a trade.

That pretty much left theft and villainy.

~*~

Shaen felt more than saw the scrawny girl slipping up behind her. Fear and hunger practically radiated off the kid. It was a sensation she'd known well back on the Asylum Ship Charity. You developed a sixth sense, a warning bell in your brain when someone was headed your way to take your stuff. It meant they were desperate enough for a fight, because fighting was severely punished on the Charity. She'd grown up on a space station that was a workhouse, orphanage and lunatic asylum rolled into one and thrown into the black endless night of space. You learned to take a lot of punishment or you died. Simple as that.

The girl's hand slipped towards the small leather bag hanging from Shaen's belt. From the corner of her eye, she saw a piece of sharp metal concealed in her hand. Whether it was to cut the purse free, or to distract her with an injury so the thief could escape, Shaen couldn't tell. Probably both, assuming the girl could think that far ahead.

As the girl's hand slid closer, Shaen pushed her smoldering drink back, grabbing the girl's wrist with her other hand. She squeezed hard and pulled forward, jerking the kid off her feet. The kid dropped the shiv to the filthy floor of the cantina. She struggled, but Shaen had weight, experience, and strength built from years of hauling crates in her favor. This girl wasn't taking Shaen's money, and she wasn't getting away until Shaen was ready to let her go.

Stringy brown hair covered a face contorted with fear and rage. Shaen pulled the girl's arm up and examined her wrist. A tattoo marked her as an emancipated orphan, or Eo. Couldn't have been much over sixteen, the youngest you could leave the ships.

"Are you dumb or just desperate, girl?" Shaen growled. "You're lucky I didn't shoot you. It's not like I couldn't smell you coming a mile off." It was true. Shaen was no stickler for hygiene herself, but the kid smelled like she hadn't bathed in a month.

"Shaen, you know there's no fighting here. You disarmed her, now either let 'er go or take her to the sheriff." Omma's weathered face offered a bitter frown.

"You don't wanna take me to the sheriff, lady. Ain't gonna be no reward. Ain't worth your time. You got me fair and square. Just let me go, and I promise I'll leave you alone. Hell, I'll leave this whole bar alone. Plenty of bars in Ghadrak."

Shaen looked into the girl's muddy brown eyes. It was tough to see them through the rat's nest of hair. She saw fear there, but also a wily intelligence. The kid wasn't just blank-eyed crazy like a lot of Eos.

She reached into her bag and plunked down the payment for her drink, never letting go of the squirming girl. The girl kicked and spat, still trying to claw Shaen's grip loose with her free hand.

"Outside, kid." She dragged the caterwauling young woman through the bar. The pair barely raised an eyebrow among the crowd. The patrons of the Drunken Monkey had seen it all. Nobody cared what one crazy woman planned to do with another.

Once they were in the alley, Shaen grabbed the girl's other shoulder and shook her. "You listening to me kid? I'm not taking you to the sheriff."

"Why?"

"First off, I hate the sheriff. Second, you're an awful thief. No point in arresting somebody who isn't even good enough to manage to steal anything."

"I can steal stuff! You'd be surprised at what I could steal!" Shaen could tell she'd injured the kid's pride.

"Fine, fine, I'm sure you're just having an off day. But at any rate, my third reason is that I might wanna offer you a job."

That stunned the kid into silence. She even stopped kicking Shaen's shins for half a second.

"You wanna what?"

"I want to offer you a job. I'm a coyote pilot. You take a mind trip on your way out of the ships?" A mind trip was common parlance for the informal entry exam for coyote pilots. You agreed to travel awake and restrained through the Passage. All Eos were offered the chance. Some were crazy enough at that point to take it. The government paid your transport ticket. In exchange, you agreed to be euthanized for the good of the state if you came out the other end a gibbering lunatic.

The girl shook her head, her eyes wide.

"I'm looking for an apprentice. If you're willing to go awake and restrained through the Passage, I'll take you on. Assuming you don't want to claw anybody's eyes out of their sockets after."

"And if I do want to claw somebody's eyes out?"

"I can airlock you or send you back to the Ships. Your choice." That was the standard agreement, but some pilots didn't want to bother with transporting a violent psychotic to the nearest UHC depot. To be fair, most Eos preferred the airlock option.

The girl appeared to be thinking it over. She bit her lip.

"You sure you're not just gonna sell me to a slaver somewhere? Why'd you wanna take on an apprentice that just tried to steal from you?"

"First of all, anybody who sells to slavers deserves what they get when they get caught. I ain't gonna say I've never transported anything illegal, but I don't work with slavers. Period. You know what happens to us, to coyote pilots, over time?"

The girl nodded.

"I don't want to end up some mindless drooling idiot someday. I take on an apprentice now, I can save up a stake. Maybe retire, sell you the ship someday. A ship all by itself is worthless without someone able to fly it. But if you get through the mind trip with your brain more or less in working order, and I show you how to fly it, we could get an investor. He'll buy the ship off me, and let you earn back the investment over time. You're pretty young. Assuming you don't gnaw off your own tongue the first trip, you could have five, maybe ten good years flying. It's a decent life, kid. A damn sight better than what you had on the Ships. Unless you think your plan to become a master thief is still a better idea?"

The girl stared at her with a mix of wonder and suspicion. Shaen knew the kid didn't have any better options, but getting that idea through to a squirrely half-crazed teenager was tough.

"Can I think about it?" The girl's voice sounded speculative.

"I'm leaving tomorrow morning. Got a jump window at 0900 hours to hit. You show up at the hangar here in town, docking bay Upsilon, if you're interested."

The girl nodded. Shaen let go of her wrist, her other hand covering her purse in case the kid was actually a much better thief than she seemed. The kid rubbed her wrist and turned away.

"Hey kid, what's your name? In case you show up tomorrow, I need to give it to the hangar guard so he'll let you pass."

"Risa," the girl called over her shoulder. "My name's Risa Sellee."

And then she ran like the devil was chasing her.

machinations

Three streets over, in a beat-up boarding house, Risa mounted the stairs two at a time. She couldn't believe her luck. It had worked! Perfectly. She hadn't even had to bring up the apprenticeship. She'd had a whole speech ready, just waiting to spill big fat crocodile tears. She was supposed to beg Morris for the chance to fly with her. Instead, Morris had brought it up like it was her own idea.

She barreled through the door into the room rented by the Vero brothers. Vahnu looked up from the card game they were playing.

"So how'd it go? You get her to agree to it?"

"Damn right I did. You picked the right woman for the job, boys. I told you." She pushed her hair back from her face, grinning wickedly at the two men.

"And she didn't suspect anything?" Vishku glared at her with dull grey eyes, the cigar clamped in his teeth dropping ash in his wiry red beard.

"Not a thing. I think she's feelin' her age, fellas. Didn't seem nearly as tough as you said she'd be."

"When you leavin'?" Vahnu frowned, like something was still bothering him about the plan. But the plan was perfect. This was the only part that left anything up to chance, and it had worked out even better than expected. Maybe that was what was bothering him. Things rarely worked out as well as he'd planned. Working out better was a first.

"She's got a jump tomorrow morning. She's gonna restrain me at first. I told her I hadn't taken a mind trip yet. Need to give her a few flights to get used to me, let down her guard."

Vishku pounded a fist on the table. "We've waited long enough, just getting your sorry arse on the same planet as her!" His wild grey eyes flashed outrage and madness. Vahnu was not sure his brother had too many good flights left in his battered brainpan.

"Look, old man! I came with you both in good faith, thinking you were offering a regular apprenticeship. I can't say I was thrilled at the idea in the first place, but I'm willing to go along with it if it means I get my own ship sooner. I could leave here, get cleaned up, find another apprenticeship where I'm not gonna have to risk life and limb, all right? I want a chance to look around that ship of hers, figure out if she's got any internal defenses, that's all. You can wait for me to earn her trust and check out her ship, or you can find a new partner!" The girl's hand were planted firmly on her hips.

Vahnu stood, walked over to her, patted her on the shoulder. "Now, don't go gettin' all flustered, Risa. We're real happy with your work so far. Vishku's just agitated, is all. He ain't got much patience. He wanted to just waltz into some bar and shoot her."

"Damn right, I did! Nobody drops me out of the sky, brother. Nobody."

"Well she did, and for all we know, she could drop you in a gunfight, too. Don't pretend you haven't considered it. Not to mention neither of us wants to end up in jail for murder. This way is better. We talked it through. Risa, here, she gets a ship. Our customer gets what she needs. We get our revenge, and a nice fat payment to boot. Enough to retire, if we want. And best of all? Shaen Morris loses everything."

preparations

Risa tried to make herself comfortable, but being strapped to a bulkhead from her shoulders to her ankles made that a challenge. It reminded her of a video she'd once seen from Old Terra, about a creature called a mummy. The Benevolence always had an ancient video playing in the common room. She couldn't imagine who thought the children aboard would benefit from watching made-up horrors from centuries past, what with the real horrors all around them. Maybe it was supposed to make Ship life seem sane in comparison.

Shaen had strapped her in as soon as she'd arrived. The cargo was already loaded. She'd evidently been there a few hours already.

"All right, then. I suppose I should ask you to pick your poison." Shaen had her goggles down and seemed to be reading something on the VR display.

"Isn't drinking liquor a bad idea right before my first flight?"

Shaen gave her a confused look. "Who said anything about liquor? That'd be stupid. You'd just throw it up the minute we were in the Passage. I'm asking you what kind of poison you'd prefer if you break down. Which is pretty likely, I won't lie.

"I've got nerve toxin, that'll take you out pretty quick. I hear it leaves a metallic taste in the mouth, though. Briefly, anyway. I've got a lethal dose of nioximeth. Takes a little longer, but supposedly you feel great until you're out. . . ."

"Shaen."

"Has to be an injection, I'm afraid. People tend not to swallow pills real well when they're in the middle of a violent mental breakdown."

"Shaen!"

"What?" Morris flashed her an innocent look through the goggles.

"Just pick whatever you think's easiest."

"Oh. Right. I guess we'll go with the nerve toxin, then. Good luck kid!" And with that, she patted Risa on the head, turned away and busied herself with getting settled in and the ship's systems fired up for take-off.

Vishku kicked his brother awake on the pallet. The infernal comm unit was flashing red again. Vahnu was pretty useless in a fight and not much better as a pilot, but Vishku had learned it was better to let his brother do the talking when it came to customers. He, himself, had an inconvenient tendency to spew random profanity and threats if he didn't like the way they looked at him. He almost never liked the way they looked at him. It tended to discourage folks from booking passage or cargo.

Vahnu grunted and rolled over, pulling himself up to a seated position.

"It's him again. You probably ought to talk to him."

Vahnu rubbed his eyes and dragged himself up into the rented room's only chair. It sat at a battered table where a small lamp flashed an intermittent red. He hit a button on the side of the lamp, and the flashing stopped.

The flashing light was replaced with the holographic image of Trenton Madaris. Or at least his head. His dark hair was streaked with grey. Even the translucence of the hologram couldn't soften the cold, calculating hardness in his eyes.

"Where do we stand with the plan, Vero? Time is running short. I'm running out of patience."

"The plan is going perfectly. Couldn't be going better." Vahnu managed a greasy smile for his client. Madaris was their hope for the future. He needed to make sure he was happy. Besides, it was the truth.

Risa had altered their plan only by a few weeks, and even he had to admit she was probably smart to be cautious. A couple extra weeks in exchange for better odds of success was a fair trade. He needed to make sure Madaris saw it that way, too.

"We've got one shot at this. If Shaen gets wind of it, we'll never get close enough to make a second attempt." He didn't add the likelihood that she'd hunt down and kill them, if she ever figured out they were involved.

"Yes, but if your plan fails, there might not be enough time to engage another suitable target." Trenton sneered at Vahnu.

"You won't need another target, sir. That's what we've been telling you. Shaen Morris is your girl. You've got a Sleeper. We've got a body."

Sleepers were a new development. They were still incredibly rare. You had to convince the UHC that you were a "significant asset to society" just to get permission to copy your synaptic patterns into a transfer unit helmet. They were tightly controlled technology. He was still impressed that Madaris and his fiancee, Jula Thayeson, wealthy and influential as they were, had managed to acquire one.

Madaris' rich lady friend Ms. Thayeson needed a new body, being as how she wore her old one out after seventy years. He may have gotten her personality and memories all zipped up in a transfer unit, but he still needed a healthy brain to download her into.

Out loud, he said, "A Sleeper's body's gotta be one that can handle . . . what was the word, again?"

"Trauma. What you and your brother are going to experience if you don't get me what I want."

"Right. Trauma. Ain't nobody's brain better suited for trauma than a coyote pilot. You know that, or like you said, no reason to talk to us . . . miscellaneous?"

"Miscreants."

"Right. Since she's yer lady friend, we're guessing you don't want her downloaded into some rough lookin' hag. I mean, you already courted an old lady for her money. No point in doing that all over again, especially when she went all terminal on ya before you could get hitched. Getting a permit to create a Sleeper must've set you both back a bit?"

Vahnu avoided speculating out loud that Jula Thayeson's matrimonial hesitation might have been insurance. Rumor had it she was a smart old coot. He doubted she'd trust Trenton Madaris to follow through on getting her a new body if he was already her husband and heir. The legal fees were astronomical, and the equipment wasn't any cheaper. Cheating death wasn't for the poor or poorly-connected.

"The cost was more than you can fathom," snapped Madaris. "Far more than it would cost to hire an assassin more competent that you or your useless brother."

Aside from the expense and difficulty of getting the equipment and permission, a Sleeper also needed consent from the current owner of her new body. Finding someone willing to be paid to have their mind deleted from their body was tougher than you might think. The units were monitored via subspace connection. If you activated one without first transmitting consent from the body donor, the UHC would stop the download.

But subspace transmissions couldn't reach ships in the Passage.

Vahnu continued, hoping he was convincing the man their plan was solid. "I'm tellin' ya, Shaen is your best bet. But she's a wily one. We need time for our girl to set things up. Otherwise, we risk blowing the whole thing."

The man frowned. "If Jula's synaptic pattern isn't downloaded into a new body by the time the probate runs out on her will, she'll be declared deceased. Her son Jeroy will inherit everything and the UHC will shut the transfer unit down remotely. Are you sure this Shaen Morris is worth the risk?"

The last complication for Sleepers was the time limit. You couldn't leave the ownership of vast fortunes in limbo forever. Sleepers had six months to find a new host body volunteer, or the UHC would power down the unit and delete them.

"She's worth it. Say what you will about Morris, she's a looker. And she's got a reputation for a sturdy brain, for one of us. Ain't never heard a complaint that she unexpectedly airlocked nobody. Ain't never gone off on a tangent and ended up on the wrong side of the galaxy. She ain't just a coyote pilot, she's one of the best. And I say that hatin' the woman's guts."

"So why are you saying it?" The man's steely eyes narrowed.

"Because going for Morris is the best plan for everybody. I ain't gonna lie. Vishku and me got our reasons for wanting her out of commission. But we've still got enough of our own marbles between us to make our way in the worlds. We'd like to keep it that way. Trust me. This is the best plan. You walk away a happy customer. Yer old lady gets downloaded into a nice young body. You pay us our fee, and we can stop flying and salvage our own brains. We screw you over with a substandard carcass for yer girlfriend? Rest easy. My brother and I already know how that'd end up."

"I still don't see why we didn't just use the Sellee girl." The man licked his lips impatiently. "She seemed attractive and healthy enough."

"Maybe. But she's also real young. Transfer might be too traumatic for her brain. Morris' brain is, shall we say, a bit more road-tested. But don't you worry none. If Shaen doesn't work out, and she doesn't kill Risa straightaway, we can always try that route. You like Risa? That's fine. She makes for a fine Plan B. Vishku and me, we'll strap 'er down, take 'er into the Passage ourselves, and try downloading Jula into her brain instead."

"And if Morris kills her? What's your plan, then?"

"We go back to where we found Risa, pick up another girl, and on her first trip through the Passage, she'll come back a whole new woman."

Trenton Madaris nodded his head. "All right, then. It seems like you have things under control. But don't mistake me. I'd appreciate adding Jula's fortune and influence to my own. I don't need it. You blow this? The two of you will be nothing but stardust and moonshine."

Vahnu smiled his greasy smile again. "You've got nothing to worry about. We've got nothing to worry about. Shaen Morris is already a dead woman walking. She just doesn't know it yet."

manipulations

"The lead ship has entered the aperture." A smoky female voice popped and crackled through the ship's ancient speakers. The Belle Starr was equipped with a Simulated Holographic Interface and Voice Activation, or SHIVA. It couldn't pilot the ship like a true artificial intelligence, but it provided the pilot with information and diagnostics.

The ship lifted off, following a UHC caravan headed to the Feldspar Outpost. It was Risa's second flight with Shaen, and her first one unrestrained. This time, Morris was going to start showing her how to fly the rusty, lobster-shaped freighter. The captain would probably still keep a wary eye on her, but at least she could move around the ship a bit more.

Risa wanted to be sure there weren't any unknown traps or self-destruct triggers. Coyote pilots were notoriously paranoid, and not just because they were usually also delusional.

Besides, once she'd disabled Shaen, she'd have to fly the ship out of the Passage on her own. The Vero brothers had trained her a bit on the general principles of flying, but she knew each ship had its own quirks. The Belle Starr was rumored to be among the quirkiest in the galaxy. She intended to learn as much as she could before she took over.

She struggled a little to split her attention between Shaen's instructions and looking for signs of booby traps. It was also tricky not letting on what she already knew. As far as Shaen was aware, she'd never set foot in the cockpit of a ship before their last trip.

She'd watched in fascination as they passed through the golden, pulsating rip formed in the lavender morning sky above Morrigan III. The UHC ships passed through just ahead of them, and they followed into the black abyss of the Passage. The rip closed behind them, and the universe blinked out.

Risa wondered if she would ever get used to the feeling. It was like a rubber band she didn't even know existed between her body and everything else just snapped. The urge to throw up was overwhelming. She felt her body go limp in the co-pilot seat and everything went white. She suspected her eyes had rolled back in her head for a second.

Shaen was just sitting there in the pilot's seat, leaning forward and flipping switches. Like she was operating a forklift in a dockside warehouse. Risa supposed that meant she'd get used to it, too, eventually.

"Hey, wanna go back in the hold, make sure everything's still strapped down okay?" Shaen was making frequent adjustments to the pitch and yaw of the ship. Physics were fairly unpredictable in the wormhole, Settings that were fine during one trip could have you spinning uncontrollably the next.

"Shouldn't I watch you, see how this part's done?" Risa asked.

"Shouldn't you shut up and let me fly this thing so we don't both die?"

"Hey! I'm supposed to be your apprentice, right? So are you planning on teaching me anything or not?"

"What's your rush, kid? You made it through the mind trip all right. I figure, first we get you used to moving around and being awake in the Passage. I'm not gonna be handing you the controls till you can go through the aperture without blacking out, for one thing. You still look like you might spew any minute, and frankly I'd rather you do it in the cargo hold than up here where I have to smell it."

"Just don't want you to think I'm planning on sitting around doing nothing. I appreciate you giving me this chance, Shaen."

Risa hoped she sounded sincere. The last thing she needed was for Shaen to get suspicious. She wanted to poke around the ship anyway. She took a few deep breaths, steadied her stomach, and then stood up. She wobbled a little, but soon got her bearings.

"I'll go check on the cargo." She slid the heavy door open between the cockpit and the hold, shutting it behind her. The motion lights activated, but it was still darker than the cockpit had been. With the door shut, she could snoop as much as she wanted. They were transporting grain from the Malachi system to the Bootlegger Nebula.

Commercial farms had a contract with the UHC to provide cheap grain for the colonies. Many farmers had discovered it was profitable to "lose" a certain portion of their harvest to fictional blights, fires or destructive animals each growing season. The "lost" grain often found its way to an emission nebula in the middle of an uninhabitable star system. The Bootlegger Nebula was home to a small collection of decommissioned generation ships outfitted with hundreds of stills and uncounted barrels of grain alcohol.

Learning the existence and location of the Bootlegger Nebula was yet another reason she was glad she'd insisted on taking a few trips with Shaen before activating the Vero brothers' plan. She was certain the two reprobates weren't going to share that kind of valuable information with her after they parted ways. Once she had possession of the Belle Starr, she still had to figure out how to earn a living with it.

"We'll do all right, the two of us, won't we, Belle?" she whispered out loud.

"You don't own this ship yet, Risa Sellee." Risa jumped and screamed. The eerie voice of the SHIVA had caught her completely off guard.

She steadied her nerves. It was only a simulated intelligence, but she'd have to be more careful. The SHIVA didn't have the intelligence to think her snooping around was suspicious behavior, or the initiative to warn its captain. Still, Shaen might have set it to perform surveillance on her when she was out of sight.

"I'm Shaen's apprentice. I'll own it eventually, right? Nothing wrong with looking forward to the future." She spoke under the assumption that anything she said would be repeated to Morris.

"If you say so. Most of your kind tries hard not to think about the future. In my admittedly limited experience."

There was something off about the voice's tone. Mainly, the fact that it had a tone. That last bit had sounded almost sarcastic. She could have sworn the first sentence had sounded like a threat. A simulated intelligence didn't emote. She wondered if the Belle's computer system had evolved into a native artificial intelligence. She'd heard that could happen. Some advanced programs could develop a personality and self-awareness. They called it ascending. The UHC developed AIs for their ship navigational systems and maintenance bots. Those machines needed some ability to think creatively and make decisions. But it was really just a series of patches and code added to the standard operating system for a ship or a robot.

She wondered if Shaen knew the freighter's computer might be a native AI. It seemed unlikely. If it was an AI and Shaen knew it, why bother getting an apprentice? Then again, she already had other pilots gunning for her because they didn't like the competition. She couldn't keep flying indefinitely. People would get suspicious.

Maybe that was it. She couldn't let people find out the ship's secret. Every coyote pilot in the galaxy would be planning to kill her and steal it. Better to get out now, before anybody suspected and tried to take her out.

Risa grinned to herself, and began checking the straps and tie-downs on the cargo. She continued to look for booby traps or self-destruct devices, but was careful to conceal her activity among the crates. If the Belle Starr had an AI on board, that could be a very lucky break. If she could win it over, she could let it pilot the ship for her. There was already a manual override switch that connected the computer to the ship's controls during flight in normal space, when an AI wasn't needed for autopilot. And as long as that switch wasn't thrown, there wasn't much the computer could do to her.

If she couldn't win the AI over, a reset would restore it to factory default. If erasing Shaen's mind was complicated, erasing the Belle's was as simple as the push of a button.

misdirection

Risa strapped herself into the co-pilot's seat, ready to leave Magha III for the second time. They'd returned after their trip to the Bootlegger Nebula to drop off some liquor and pick up more cargo.

She'd picked up the transfer unit from Vahnu after telling Shaen she needed to grab her few belongings from a storage unit before the rental expired and they tossed them in the streets. Like all the best lies, it benefitted from being 90% truth. She'd brought the helmet aboard stuffed in a huge duffel with everything else she owned. While Shaen dealt with the cargo customer out in the warehouse, she'd stashed it in one of the storage compartments in the cockpit. Time to finish what she'd started.

Her feelings were surprisingly mixed. She told herself it was because she wanted a little more time to learn from Morris. But truth was, Shaen was sort of growing on her. She wasn't exactly a warm, motherly type, but neither of them would know what to do with somebody like that, anyway. Shaen had an off-kilter charm, and even seemed protective of her, in her own way.

Earlier this week, they'd been getting a meal at the Drunken Monkey. A thug had tried to grab Risa as they passed through the cantina. Before his hand made contact with her backside, Shaen had pulled one of her pistols on him.

"She's with me, Prestridge." The man had jerked his hand back like Risa's ass was a chemical fire. He'd rubbed a jagged scar on his other arm and glared at Morris. Apparently, it wasn't their first encounter. But he didn't bother either of them again.

Shaen wasn't exactly a mama bear. She was more like a slightly brain-damaged guard dog. After their last flight, Shaen had dubbed Risa "only slightly more bonkers than before we left" and it almost felt like a compliment.

They were flying to Oberon, a class M planet. The UHC classified worlds according to their technological ceiling, as opposed to any aspect of the planet itself like temperature, terrain or ecology. The UHC didn't bother classifying uninhabitable worlds. The ones you could colonize got sorted according to what kind of goods and services you could produce, sell, and most importantly, tax.

Some colonists preferred an agrarian, pre-industrial class A world. Low pollution and a simple life, but you couldn't take anything more complicated than a wind-up toy off the spaceport. Class I worlds like Magha had industrial development: diesel, steam, coal, or whatever alien rock they could get to burn powered the factories there. Class E worlds had an electronic infrastructure, similar to the old Terra of the 21st century.

Oberon was a class M, which meant they produced advanced materials. The production of conductive polymers, graphene, metamaterials and nanomaterials meant that class M worlds had the most advanced technology, along with the greatest wealth in the galaxy.

Risa checked the hold and made sure everything was secured. She was barely nauseous. It was surprising how fast she'd gotten accustomed to the weird feeling of disconnection that pervaded the Passage. She returned to the cockpit, and slid into the co-pilot's seat.

"Don't make it out to a class M all that often," said Shaen. "They generally don't have a lot of use for nonofficial transport. Well, except for Oberon."

Risa shifted in her seat uncomfortably. This was the trip. She was going to have to take out Morris and steal the ship.

She'd put off the Vero brothers as long as she could. If she didn't go through with it, they'd hunt her down and make her pay for it. Once she did what she had to do, there'd be no more asking Shaen for helpful career advice. She had been soaking up as much information as she could these last few weeks.

"Why's Oberon different?" she asked.

"Well, it's not like Ashada or some of the more hoity-toity class M planets out there. No art galleries and architectural wonders. Oberon might have a charter for advanced materials, but they also have the laxest restrictions on experimentation in the galaxy. The UHC pretty much keeps their hands off the mad scientists on Oberon. It's where people go when their project would be illegal or impossible somewhere else."

"Which means there's a healthy smuggling trade?" Risa smirked.

"Which means they're our kind of people," Shaen confirmed, nodding.

"So what are we picking up"? Risa tried to keep her voice light.

Shaen paused, taking a deep breath. "I try not to ask. And you better not, either. A curious smuggler has an even shorter than average life expectancy."

The convoy floated ahead of them, tracing an erratic path through the Passage towards the coordinates where the exit aperture would appear. It looked like it might be a relatively uneventful trip, aside from Risa's planned treason, assault and psychic murder.

The last trip, Shaen had to break out the electrical harpoons to fend off what looked like a school of interstellar jellyfish made of molten lava. They'd also had to take evasive maneuvers when the SHIVA had spotted something it called a "tuathu storm." Risa didn't know what that was, but something about Morris' body language as she'd adjusted course told her she was glad she didn't get a visual.

So far, it was a quiet flight. The official transport convoy they were following was easily in sight. That was the first lesson. Never lose sight of your piggyback. The only way in or out of the Passage was through the apertures the UHC punched through the fabric of reality for their official transports. They usually didn't object to coyote ships following along, as long as they didn't endanger the official ships. But they wouldn't hold the door open for one, either. Losing track of the ship that brought you in meant you risked losing your way back out. Falling off course for more than a few minutes could mean being trapped in the twisted purgatory of the Passage forever.

Risa knew she was running out of time. Once the lead ship cracked open the exit aperture, they would only have moments before they were out of the Passage and back in normal space. The exchange had to take place here, where there was no subspace communication possible. She had to act quickly.

"I'm going to grab a sweater. It's kinda cold in here."

Risa stood and slipped back a few steps, silently opening the storage compartment. She pulled out a metal skullcap. Copper prongs jutted out at six points around its perimeter. Indicator lights and electrodes covered the outer surface. Shaen appeared to be absorbed in thought, operating the controls of the ship. Her goggles were down, which meant the top of her head was fully exposed. Risa just needed to slip behind her and slap the cap down as hard as she could. The clamps would engage, Shaen would be paralyzed in a stasis field, and the unit would start the process of deleting her fractured mind. After her body was wiped clean of her memories and personality, it would download Jula's electronically recorded consciousness. The device would rewire Shaen's synaptic pathways to match the recording of Jula's. In every way that mattered, Shaen Morris would cease to exist.

That was the deal she'd made. The Vero brothers had been paid to find a replacement body. Risa's part was to get close to Morris and perform the swap. In the Passage, there was no chance of Morris sending a signal out to contradict Risa's story. The transfer couldn't be shut down, even without a donor consent. She'd claim that Shaen had volunteered, and left the ship to her. With Jula safely ensconced in Shaen's body, they were counting on her power and money to help keep the real story quiet. It didn't hurt that the UHC wouldn't want anyone discovering a Sleeper had figured out a way around their safeguards. If word got out that a rich CEO had successfully hijacked a new body without consent, there'd be anarchy. They just needed a halfway plausible story, and no obvious evidence to prove it wasn't true.

She slipped up towards Shaen, one hand extended with the transfer unit. It was now or never.

Her hand was raised above Shaen's head when the metal plate beneath her feet pulsed with a jolt of electricity. It knocked her unconscious even through her boots. She dropped to the floor, the transfer unit clattering to the floor beside her.

~*~

"I've contained the threat. Feel free to thank me at any time." The disembodied voice of the ship echoed through the cabin.

"Cut it kinda close there, didn't ya, Belle?" Shaen had leapt from the pilot's seat. "I hope that jolt didn't fry the transfer unit."

"Captain?" A slight inflection indicated Shaen was forgetting something important.

"Oh, right." Shaen threw a large metal switch, coupling the computer that held Belle's nascent AI to the navigational controls. "You're now in control of the ship, Belle. Try not to wreck it."

"I'll do what I can, Shaen," sarcasm dripped from the popping and crackling simulated voice.

Shaen had neither the time nor the social awareness to take umbrage. She plucked the transfer unit from the floor. Tapping a few buttons on the console nearby brought a holographic image fluttering to life in the center of the cabin. The translucent image of a young man flickered a few times before stabilizing.

"Good! It looks like your friend Yuri's experimental device works." Jeroy Thayeson, oldest son and heir of Jula, rubbed his hands together. "What did he call it? A quantum entanglement projector?"

"Don't ask me, Thayeson. I'm not the mad genius. I'm just the bait." Shaen barked at the hologram.

"Yes, yes. I understand you're stressed. It's just gratifying to have promises of a technological miracle actually pan out for once. You've no idea how much money I've sunk into experimental vaporware—"

"Maybe not, but I do have an idea of how much time we've got here before I have to get this ship out of the Passage."

"Oh! Right. Of course. Please bring the transfer unit to the camera." Shaen picked up the helmet, and took it to the small lens concealed at the back of the cockpit.

"I can't see it clearly, Captain Morris. But there should be a digital display with a unique PIN number. Please read it to me."

Shaen rattled off the numbers that glowed green on the display. Jeroy checked them against a datapad in his hand.

"That's my mother's imprint, all right. Sorry, I just needed to be sure. Now find the power button. I need to see you power the unit down fully." Shaen pressed the button, holding it close to the lens as the flickering lights died, and with them, the digital copy of Jula Thayeson's memories.

"Perfect, captain. As soon as you emerge from the Passage, the UHC will register my mother as officially deceased. The estate will be taken out of probate, and you'll receive your payment as soon as I receive my inheritance."

"I'd better, Jeroy. Unless you want the UHC to know your mother was planning to hijack my body. They'd just love to show that nobody, not even the rich and powerful, can pull one over on the government."

"You don't need to worry, Shaen. I'm a man of my word. You'll have your payment."

"Good. Now I'm turning this blasted thing off. Keeping this miracle running is draining my ship's engines faster than a colonist drains a beer. Consider your cargo delivered safely to Oberon." She stalked over to the console.

"Speaking of cargo, what do you plan to do with the—" with two taps of a button, he disappeared.

"Belle? How are we looking?"

The speakers crackled to life. "So far, so good. No sign of the exit aperture yet, and I've kept us perfectly in sync with the convoy."

"Yes, I'm sure you're an exemplary pilot. Great. I'm calling Yuri."

"Shaen! We don't have time. Or the engine reserves!"

"We don't if you keep arguing with me. I'm doing this, Belle."

Shaen tapped the console buttons again, and the holographic channel flickered to life once more. This time, the ghost in her cockpit was a compact man in his early forties. Thick, greying dreadlocks fell over the collar of his grimy lab coat. Wire-rimmed glasses sat perched on his nose.

"Mad Yuri!"

"Shaen Morris! You're a fine one to call somebody mad. Have you got it?"

"Right here." She lifted the transfer helmet towards the lens. "What do I do?" Shaen hoped she'd be able to understand him through the massive interference created by trying out experimental and theoretically improbable quantum holography.

"Power the unit back on." She pressed the button and held it, and the unit flickered on, various lights and LEDs blinking across its surface.

"Okay, here's the fun part. Slap it on the girl's head, as hard as you can."

Shaen pulled the unconscious Risa up into her lap. She raised her hand, and plonked the transfer unit onto the girl's skull. The clamps bit down.

"Now what?" The girl's body stiffened and flattened out like a board. Shaen wiggled out from under her.

"There should be an upload button."

"This?"

"No! That's the eject button, Shaen! The one to the right of it."

"This?"

"Yes! Hit it now!"

Shaen pressed the blue button, and the metal skullcap hummed. The lights on top blinked faster.

"All right, now. You should be good."

The voice of the Belle piped in. "That's good, because we've got our window. Time to get back to reality, Shaen."

Shaen slapped the buttons on the console, killing the holograph. She jumped into the pilot's seat, slamming the switch back to disengage the AI from the navigational controls. Up ahead, just in front of the lead ship of the convoy, a golden rip appeared in the fabric of the universe.

They popped out of the Passage and back into normal space. Shaen had a clear visual of Oberon. She opened a normal communications channel to Yuri on the planet's surface.

"Caravel class cargo ship Belle Starr to Nicholas Labs."

Yuri's voice crackled over the official channels. "Go ahead Belle Starr. This is Nicholas Labs, Yuri Nicholas speaking."

"I'm approaching Oberon with your cargo. Please transmit landing coordinates and permissions to Oberon ATC."

"Very good." If anyone was listening from the UHC, it would be impossible to tell from their tone that the two had just been yelling frantically at each other only minutes earlier.

Or, for that matter, that they'd known each other for years before this cargo assignment.

consecration

"A toast! To your first, and hopefully last, apprentice!"

Shaen lifted her glass reluctantly. She didn't much like vodka, but Yuri had insisted. Then again, there wasn't much about this whole situation she did like.

As soon as they'd landed, Yuri had been waiting with a maglev gurney and some medical equipment. The two of them had lifted the board-stiff Risa and slid her onto the gurney. Then Yuri had taken over, while Shaen went about the business of scrubbing the ship down. Jeroy had warned her that it was possible his mother's paramour, a man named Trenton Madaris, might contest the will. If that was the case, the UHC might come sniffing around the ship, looking for evidence of foul play. A full forensic scrub was in order. Shaen was cleaning out the physical evidence; the Belle was flushing out any digital traces.

However, since Madaris had been planning on illegally hijacking a body for his Sleeper, the odds were he'd leave well enough alone. An investigation into the "accidental" power loss on Jula's unit might uncover more than Madaris wanted found. In fact, Shaen and Jeroy had left a trail pointing straight to him in the event of any investigation into Jula's premature (or belated, depending on how you looked at it) demise. Even if he could prove they'd deliberately powered down the unit a month before probate ended, that still wouldn't make him her heir. His chances of claiming Jula's fortune had been erased right along with her neural copy. He had nothing to gain and much to lose by outing them. Still, it paid to be careful.

"So you think she's okay in there?" Shaen swirled the cocktail in her glass. Vodka and the tangy-sweet juice of some red berry native to Oberon. It wasn't bad. It wasn't quite as flammable as her usual libations, but it wasn't bad, either.

"I'm as sure as I can be. I got her body into stasis before we removed the transfer unit. The initial diagnostics I ran looked clean. The girl's body is fine. Her mind is fine, as far as I can tell. She just has a digital backup of the latter now."

"And you think you can restore that backup to her body?"

"Well, if I can't, we've pretty much done all this for nothing, haven't we? But yes, I have every reason to believe we can use the transfer unit technology to create the rollback helmet. Risa will be our first test subject. We upload her pattern to the server, save a copy, and download it back into her original body, using the duplicate helmet I'm building. Worst case scenario, it doesn't work and we just wake her up from stasis. Best case, we've figure out a way to hold off mental deterioration, maybe indefinitely."

Shaen had known Yuri for years, ever since shortly after the incident that had gotten him dubbed "Mad Yuri." He'd been a scientist and brilliant researcher before. Not the sort of man who'd have any need for a smuggler like Shaen. Then during a routine Passage flight between worlds, a creature from the depths of the void had attacked his ship. The AI had tried evasive maneuvers, but failed.

Protocol demanded that passengers were awakened, one at a time, to see if any of them could take over and save the ship. Yuri had been the fourth one awakened. He was the first one the AI didn't have to immediately subdue. He had nearly tripped over the remains of their bodies, before frantically attempting a blind jump. Most UHC ships were equipped with a device that could create a small exit aperture. But there was no telling where the ship would come out in normal space.

Yuri had been exceptionally lucky. He'd managed to escape the creature, and then send out a subspace distress signal. A rescue ship was able to plot a jump to their coordinates. He'd escaped with his life. And most of his mind, which was a miracle. But his reputation as a scientist had been irrevocably lost.

He had been diagnosed with degenerative mental disease due to exposure to the Passage. The doctors at the recovery facility told him that in his case, it looked as though the disease progression would resemble senile dementia. It would possibly progress slower than patients of average intelligence, but over time, he would lose his most valuable asset. His remarkable mind.

It was a heavy blow when he lost his prestigious position with a well-known biotech corporation on Ashada. But not as heavy as the realization that it would be difficult for him to find work of any kind, once an employer learned of his experience.

That was when Shaen met him. He needed transport to Oberon. He'd realized his best opportunity was working at the fringes of science and research. On Oberon, the scientists were all a little mad. He'd found a research facility that was willing to overlook his condition. With time, he believed he could once again head his own lab and make a contribution to humanity.

They'd kept in touch. Yuri always hired Shaen for cargo runs whenever possible. Yuri was one of the few people Shaen trusted with her life.

It was surprisingly hard to trust him with someone else's.

"Okay, Doc. I believe you'll do your best. If I didn't trust you, you wouldn't have been the first person I contacted when I got wind of the Vero brothers'... unique career opportunity." She smirked a little over her glass. Vahnu and Vishku were going to have their hands full, explaining to Madaris that they'd lost his rich girlfriend's mind.

"How did you get wind of that whole imbroglio, if you don't mind my asking?" Yuri leaned forward, his ruddy brown skin lit by the glow of the coal furnace that warmed the sitting room outside his laboratory.

"The real heir. Jeroy Thayeson. Evidently, he suspected that Trenton Madaris' interest in his septuagenarian mother was less about her sparkling personality and more about her obscene fortune. When the months dragged on and Madaris wasn't able to find a consenting donor, Jeroy figured he might get desperate. He paid for any information related to his mother or Madaris for weeks, and finally got a hit. He probably knew the Vero brothers had the job, and what the job really was, before they did. He contacted all the female coyote pilots they were known to have a grudge against. It's a short but distinguished list, and I'm at the top of it."

"And that's when you contacted me?"

"Right. I knew you were looking for a transfer unit on the black market, and having no luck. I figured if Madaris was looking for a body, and the Veros had volunteered me, I might be able to get my hands on one for you."

"Smart girl. So, when Risa showed up?"

"I already figured Vahnu and Vishku wouldn't go after me directly. Honestly, if she was as bad a thief as she pretended to be on Magha, she'd have been dead already. I spotted her for a plant pretty much right off the bat."

"Well, it's good for both of us you were right. And good that the quantum holography worked. By the way, I'm now in talks with Jeroy Thayeson to mass produce them. This has turned out to be quite the profitable game, Shaen. For both of us."

"It's only begun, Doc. If you get that rollback helmet working, it's not just going to make us both a fortune. It's going to change everything for the Eos and coyote pilots out there."

"Yes. It's sort of suspicious that the UHC hasn't put the technology to that use already. It stands to reason, if you can make a perfect copy of someone's neural pattern, you can create a 'saved version' of their mind. In the case of degenerative mental diseases like yours and mine, you can halt the progression of the disease! Imagine it, Shaen."

"I'll believe it when I see it, Doc. Let's start with getting Risa's mind synced back up with her body. But if it works. . . . Well, Doc, there aren't words for what that'd mean. Not just for me. For so many people."

"It's not a perfect solution, Shaen. You'll have to download memories periodically, or else you'll lose them when you restore your mind to the save point."

"I understand that, Doc. But it's hope. It's more than I had before."

"You could have just let the Belle fly for you."

"That's what Belle said. But that's a temporary fix, and you both know it. If I kept flying, someone would've figured it out eventually. Legends have a short life expectancy, Yuri. I don't know if you've noticed that. My life wouldn't have been worth a plug nickel with that plan. But this way, everybody gets to keep flying. At least, anybody competent enough to afford your helmet, which'll be a lot of folks. And nobody has a reason to steal my ship and kill me for it."

"That's what I love about you, Shaen. You're smart enough to not screw yourself over by looking out for only your own interests. A lot of otherwise smart men over the years have failed to grasp the wisdom of that strategy." He lifted his glass in a toast to her. "So, you get the first unit, and a percentage profit once we've completed testing and start rolling them out for real. Is there anything else you want from this? I mean, you did take the biggest risk."

Shaen tilted her head a minute, considering things. Yes, she'd taken a big chance, but the risk of doing nothing had been much greater. She had no regrets about taking on this particularly complicated job.

Well, there was one other thing she wanted.

~*~

Yuri stabilized the camera. Shaen's instructions had been clear. Record this video, and play it back for Risa as soon as she woke up with her mind back in her own body.

Shaen sat in Yuri's overstuffed armchair. She looked straight into the camera, imagining it was the eyes of the girl she'd come to like, despite her bad intentions. She reminded her too damn much of herself not to like her, at least a little.

"Hello there, kid. If you're seeing this, it means you're awake and okay. You may have taken a little trip first, but I did what I could to make sure you got back to something like normal. That's a hell of a lot more than you were going to do for me.

"You made a mistake trusting the Vero brothers. And an even bigger one thinking you could steal the Belle Starr from me. I suspect you know that, now. If you don't, you're not as smart as I thought.

"You might be worried that I plan to take revenge for what you were gonna do. But I'm leaving you with a way to make things square between us. When you get back, I want you to find Vahnu and Vishku. And I want you to tell them that the next time they screw with me, I will end them."

Shaen smiled as Yuri turned off the camera. It was time to get back to her ship.

She had a future to plan.

Episode 3:
The Belly of the Beast

70

THE BELLY OF THE BEAST

stranded

Drevin suppressed a smile as he surveyed his cards. He'd drawn a sage of ships to complete the royal fleet he'd been working towards, discarding the five of settlers.

He'd taken up gambling after his brief foray into selling stolen goods went coreward thanks to a botched delivery. He took on the occasional mercenary gig, too. Plenty of ways to make a living in the wide expanse of space, if you were smart, aggressive, and less than honest.

Right now, though, most of his entrepreneurial efforts were on hold. He'd been stuck in the Bootlegger Nebula for over a week, along with half the smugglers in the galaxy and their passengers. Nobody knew why the government portals out of the Passage had quit opening, and nobody knew when or if they'd start back up.

No harm in making bank off the boredom in the meantime.

He was laying down his cards when the ale room hatch swung open. A familiar head of spiky white-blond hair poked through, crowned with a beat-up pair of mechanic's goggles.

Not her again.

Drevin gathered his winnings from the hand as the other players swiveled to look, hoping for fresh meat at the tables. One man snorted in recognition. Shaen Morris, pilot of the Belle Starr, had a reputation.

She hadn't changed. Same grubby trench covered a greasy tank top and canvas pants with a half-dozen pockets and pouches. She still wore the same heavy mag-boots.

Still carried the same enormous pistol slung low on her utility belt.

The last time he'd seen her, he'd slipped out, hoping to escape her notice. This time, he wasn't leaving until he was good and done playing cards. Besides, it wasn't like he could get far. At best, he could shuttle from the Lee Petty to another ship in the Bootlegger's fleet of distilleries.

Hell, she might not even remember him. She was a smuggler, and they were all insane. She flew through the Passage awake, and everybody knew time passed strangely there. From her point of view, it could have been years since Mebarik.

He decided to ignore her and finish the game.

~*~

Shaen Morris had been trapped in the Bootlegger Nebula for nine days, 12 hours and 33 minutes, and she hadn't killed anybody yet.

It might have been due to her recent partial thaw towards humanity after a lifetime of misanthropy. More likely, it was the near-limitless supply of cheap whiskey. It certainly wasn't because she enjoyed staying in one place too long, especially the Nebula.

On one hand, the Bootleggers were relatively self-sufficient. The fleet of reconditioned generation ships still had oxygen and nutrient gardens. Aside from reclamation, they harvested water from a comet some enterprising folks had towed into the vicinity. They also had a hell of a lot of booze, since that was the point of a Bootlegger Nebula in the first place.

But the whole thing reminded Shaen too much of the Asylum ship she'd grown up on — a floating orphanage, poorhouse, prison, mental asylum and nursing home, all rolled into one miserable place. She'd kept to the Belle, only leaving to visit the public ale rooms to drink, play cards or engage in whatever commerce could be had among the stranded smugglers and their illegal — and highly irritable — passengers.

She'd rather be on the Belle now, but she had a meeting with Chenaux Kaki, an old contact who claimed he had a job for her once the portals started running again. Not much point in planning for what would happen if they didn't open up soon. Chaos would erupt as patience gave out and hair-trigger tempers finally exceeded the booze's ability to numb them.

The cacophony of noise and flashing blue-green light of the ale room bled into the corridor behind her. Shaen prepared herself for the sensory assault as she climbed through the open hatch. The smell of sour mash, spoiled vegetation and sweat permeated the whole ship, but the ale rooms reeked of it.

She scanned the room, looking for Chenaux. For a moment, she thought she spied him playing cards, then realized it was just a guy she'd turned down for a fare a couple years ago on Mebarik.

She grinned, remembering the odd cargo she'd picked up instead that day: an android named Whiskey, and Ward, the orphan he had rescued from a fire. She'd dropped the pair off on an island in the N'Bari system, where they were faring well. She tried to check in with them every few standard months to make sure they were stocked up on supplies. If this situation didn't change soon, she worried about what might happen to them.

Movement caught her eye: Chenaux waving her over. She ambled through the crowd and slid into a creaky chair across from the generally agreeable miscreant.

She leaned back and twitched two fingers, signaling the server for a drink. Ismael made a rude gesture in return. He clearly wasn't bringing anything till Shaen verified she had credits to pay. Shaen tapped a pattern on the side of her goggles, and her name popped up in green pixels in a display over the bar.

"Chenaux. I hear you've got cargo, once the Unis get the portals back up and running."

"And I hear your ship still hasn't rattled to pieces." Chenaux flashed a wide, wicked grin before popping a roasted rachnut into his mouth. His healthy girth marked him as a moderately successful fence. An amiable nature and modest ambition let him escape the notice of the UHC and more carnivorous members of the underworld. His gift was an unerring sense of what was within his grasp and what to leave on the table.

Shaen called out her drink order to Ismael, and then leaned across the table to be heard over the noise. Unlike most places, at least you didn't have to worry about the authorities overhearing you in the Nebula. "So where is it, where do you need it to be, and how fast does it have to get there?"

Chenaux shifted in his seat and nodded toward the aft bulkhead. "A cargo bay over on the Bill McCoy, but don't let that worry ya. I'll get it shuttled over and hauled to your usual docking bay. Gotta get it to N'Bari system. Sooner would be better than later — not that we have a lot of control over that at the moment."

"Seems simple enough." She pulled her goggles down and tapped open an audio link to Belle. "How much space we got in the hold?"

The speakers in her goggles crackled to life. "We've got one bay full of Yuri's stock, and another full of provisions. The other cargo, you've sold off already."

"So four bays open? Thanks, Belle." Shaen flipped the goggles back up to her head. "That work for you?"

"Yeah, that'll be fine. To be honest, I was surprised to learn you were still taking cargo. From what I hear, you've got something a lot bigger going." Kaki rubbed his forehead before taking a swig of his drink.

"So you've heard about Yuri and my little side business, eh?" Shaen leaned back, folding her arms across her chest.

The fence smirked. "Are you kidding? Every pilot who still has half a brain left either has one or is saving up to buy it."

About a year ago — Shaen wasn't great at measuring time — she had "acquired" some experimental tech the rich used to copy their memories and personality into a new body after death. Her friend Yuri had reverse-engineered it into what they called a rollback helmet. Smugglers could use it to literally save whatever mind they had left, by "re-installing" it every so often. They'd lose memories of the time in-between, but if it meant they could avoid a psychotic break, they could keep a damn scrapbook.

Kaki smirked at her across the table. "So why are you still out there hauling crates, when you could be sitting back collecting credits?"

Shaen shrugged. "Money don't change what I am, and that's a pilot. Plus, it's not like we've got a shipping permit. How do you figure we move 'em?" She winked at the old reprobate.

"So you're the boss and mail room clerk?"

"I'm not the boss. Yuri's the brains. Obviously."

Ismael plunked a mug full of green foaming brew on the table. Shaen nodded at him.

Kaki gave her a skeptical look. "Surely there's somebody you'd trust to handle delivery?"

Shaen frowned at him, taking a slow sip of matcha milk stout, smacking her lips and licking the green foam off the edge of the mug. The Bootleggers made beer, whiskey, gin, rum or vodka from whatever surplus — or stolen — foodstuffs they could get their hands on, including powdered green tea. Not her favorite, but not the worst thing ever.

"I appreciate the concern. But the best thing about this deal is it lets me keep flying."

"Yeah, you would say that. Already too damn crazy for that gadget to help, ain't ya?"

Shaen cackled with laughter. "Yeah. Something like that. Thanks for worrying. But I'm a big girl. I can take care of myself."

She gulped another mouthful of beer as Kaki transmitted the details of the job from his gauntlet to her goggles, which she pulled down to scan. It was a solid arrangement, and it gave her an excuse to work in a quick visit with Whiskey and Ward. She looked up and noticed the guy from Mebarik headed for the hatch.

"Hey, Greaseball!" she called out. "Glad to see you got off that rock okay, after all." Her moods were mercurial, and this meeting had boosted her spirits. She nodded in the gambler's direction as he eyed her with surprise then offered an uneasy grin.

"Yeah, no thanks to you, Nutjob." His tone was cautiously friendly.

"That's what you get for pinning your hopes on a coyote." She slugged the rest of her beer, and watched the folks playing cards. The greaseball shook his head, laughed and headed out the hatch.

stumped

Shaen glared at her cards. After her chat with Chenaux, she'd joined a card game. She held a pair of aces: soldiers and supplies. The rest of her hand was a random assortment of settlers and ships. Like her current situation and the macha milk stout, not the worst hand, but not a great one, either.

She tapped open a channel to Belle. "Any word from Yuri?"

The man across from her, a coyote named Darius, rolled his eyes. She shot him a glare.

A voice crackled through the tinny speaker. "Nothing yet, Boss. Sorry."

She discarded and drew two cards, and tapped off the comm.

The draw was a waste of time.

"Anybody else try to hail their piggyback when it went AWOL?" Lorsa, a smuggler sitting to Shaen's right, scratched her nose. It was either a tell or an allergy.

Darius nodded as he dropped two discards. "Not that it did any good. Not like they've ever responded to us, even before they all decided to veer off course and strand us in the nothing."

Lorsa shrugged. "Yeah, it was a long shot, but I figured maybe if it was a malfunction, they'd be willing to accept our help." The redhead discarded one card, and the ghost of a smile passed her face as she slid its replacement into her hand.

Shaen laughed. "And admit their ships aren't perfect models of efficiency? Not likely."

"It wasn't a malfunction." Raj, an older pilot, sorted the cards in his hand. No discard.

Shaen bit her lip. Raj had been around a while. Long enough to have picked up an android named Sierra Mike, who served as mechanic and first mate on the Prisha.

"How would you know?" Darius tossed another chip into the pot.

Shaen sighed. "It wasn't a malfunction. It was a signal. The AIs were responding to a rogue signal in the Passage."

Raj glanced over at her and nodded, once. "We . . . picked up on it, too." He pulled his cards closer, and she noticed a bruise on his wrist. The clean, sharp edges matched a maintenance android's hand grip.

Huh. "Picking up on it." That was one way to put it.

She was gradually getting used to the idea that the Simulated Holographic Interface and Voice Activation, or SHIVA, which ran most of the Belle's automatic systems had "ascended" and become a true AI. Over the years, she'd grown accustomed to the ship's vocal simulator and its scratchy pops and clicks. She'd even gotten used to the snarky tone it had developed once Belle became self-aware.

She was still not prepared to hear it produce an ear-piercing, horrified scream. Or to have to rush over and switch all systems to manual control. She had not been prepared for the eerie, absolute silence, which continued until they left the Passage through the Bootlegger's portal — the one portal not controlled by the Unis, which always opened at regular intervals.

Before she could lay down her hand, a fight broke out at the next table. She and the others abandoned their game to avoid getting sucked into the fray. The fragile camaraderie of their unexpected exile had begun to deteriorate.

She sidled towards the hatch, mostly trying to avoid the brawl. When one idiot was dumb enough to grab her arm, she bloodied his nose with the butt of her pistol grip.

Pulling herself free and almost tumbling out of the ale room, she headed out into the rabbit warren of corridors, freshly reminded why she usually avoided people.

Blinking lights led down a grimy corridor from the ale room back to her hangar bay on delta deck. A thick fug of smoke carrying the scent of machine oil, grain alcohol and sweat hung over the dim passageway. She pulled down her goggles and scanned the VR display, confirming she was headed the right way. Directional signage left a lot to be desired in the flotilla. Shaen figured it was by design. Being tough to find was a Bootlegger goal in general.

The Nebula was easy enough to find on star charts, but didn't merit exploration. With no habitable worlds nearby, there was no good reason to go there. It was the perfect place to park a few dozen generation ships and commence producing untaxed booze.

Getting the centuries-old ships habitable was easy — the hard part had been bribing and blackmailing a renegade tech firm to build them a portal in and out of the Passage. The Unis were a bureaucracy, and where there's bureaucracy, there are people willing to sell classified information. The Bootleggers managed to get manifests regularly, letting them know when official transports were due to arrive and open portals back out to the various worlds where their product would find a home.

Right now, Shaen was grateful for the Bootleggers' enterprising spirit — or enterprise of spirits, as the case may be. Otherwise, she'd still be trapped in the Passage.

After her conversation at the card table, she was convinced something new and horrifying lurked within the eldritch wormhole — and, considering the monsters she'd run into during what passed for "normal" conditions, that was saying something.

She wound her way back to the Belle, trying to avoid the most run-down parts of the Lee Petty. But the ship was over three hundred years old, and it looked every day of it, and she wasn't that familiar with the place.

Most smugglers stopped by the Bootlegger Nebula in between jobs. The distillers always had a shipment ready to go.

But it was boring work, and Shaen had a low tolerance for boredom. She didn't know its twists and turns as well as some others did.

A lot of young pilots spent a year or so doing nothing but earning their "whiskey wings." So it shouldn't have been surprising when Shaen ran into one she'd rather have avoided.

The last time she'd seen Risa Sellee, the girl was an empty shell. She'd gotten caught in her own trap, a plot to give a dead billionaire Shaen's body. The kid was more pawn than player. Which was mostly why Shaen had asked Yuri to put her digitally-archived mind back where it belonged — after Shaen was long gone.

Risa might be grateful her mind hadn't been deleted. She might be mad about her mind getting sucked out of her body. Or she could be crazy after weeks stored on a hard drive. Shaen wasn't dying to find out which of those options it would be.

The girl's frown turned to a look of pure fear, prompting Shaen to remember she'd threatened to kill her if she ever saw her again. She had been angry at the time.

Risa ducked, turned, and knocked over three people as she fled.

Right. Mortal terror is another possibility.

Shaen's eyes narrowed. Something didn't quite add up. She could have sworn the girl had been heading toward her. Her frown had seemed more determination than dislike. The fear hadn't seemed aimed at Shaen.

Something solid thudded against her shoulder from behind. She caught a glimpse of a woman in hammered bronze body armor, pushing her way through the crowd. Maybe she was what caused Risa to reverse thrusters like the devil himself was after her.

Noticing the sinister runes marked across the back of the merc's helmet, she thought Risa had the right idea. Shaen had never met Kai-Anne Cerrano, but the bounty hunter's distinctive armor was unmistakable. She had long since passed the point where stealth held a greater advantage than the terror of her reputation.

If Risa was on Cerrano's hit list, she'd landed in an even worse situation than having her mind deleted. One of the rules Shaen followed — in lieu of having reliable judgment — was to stay out of any trouble she could avoid. Even if the trouble seemed like fun. Getting between the baddest bounty hunter in the black and her quarry did not seem like much fun.

She turned and headed down a narrow corridor toward the Belle. The flotilla felt claustrophobic. She hated burning the fuel required to open a quantum channel, but it was time to call Yuri. If anyone living someplace that officially existed knew what was going on — and more importantly, when it would end — it would be him.

THE BELLY OF THE BEAST

confounded

"Where in the hell have you been, woman?"

Even through the watery quantum hologram, Shaen could tell Yuri's dark features were pulled into a stern expression under dreadlocks threaded with grey. His faint Russian accent was more pronounced than usual — a sure sign he'd been worried.

"In the Bootlegger Nebula. Where did you expect me to go, once the Uni ships went off-course in the Passage and stopped opening portals?" She ran her fingers through her hair, feeling a small lump at the back of her skull where she'd gotten bumped around during the fracas at the ale room.

"Of course, of course. Not all of us are privy to the inner workings of the smuggling trade."

Yuri was the typical mad scientist. If he considered it interesting — like brain chemistry and electronics — he could rattle off information all day. And often did. But his awareness of mundane things left a lot to be desired.

"So, have the Unis released a statement? I assume the populace has noticed all transit skidding to a sudden stop?" If Yuri didn't know anything, Shaen might be the one person in the universe who knew the most about what had happened.

And if that was the case, the universe was really screwed.

"Naturally, but it's all bullshit and hand-waving. Good luck discerning anything of value. What's more interesting is what they're planning to do about it."

"Why do I feel like this is more bad news?" Shaen kicked rhythmically against the bulkhead, trying to burn off the anxious energy this call had already prompted.

Thump. Thump. Thump.

"When is anything the Unis do good news?" Yuri rubbed his face, then seemed to remember they were burning through the Belle's fuel cells. "Shaen, they've made their own rollback helmet."

"What? Why the hell would they do that?"

"Because they need pilots. They don't know much, but they've pieced together that the problem is their AI navs. The next logical step is to revert to human pilots. . . ."

"And we've conveniently given them a way to make that possible. Shit." Her bulkhead kicking increased in pace.

Thump-thump-thump-thump.

"Boss! Quit kicking my guts." Belle couldn't be hurt, but it was shocking how easily she could get annoyed.

"There is some good news. They're going to start opening the portals twice a day. I think they hope the smugglers show up, so they can make their pitch for the Clean Start Program."

"Do I even want to know what this Clean Start Program is?"

"Probably. Sounds like we're going to have a big competitor, if we aren't driven out of business entirely. And you might want to consider their offer. But you have to be running low on auxiliary power. We can take this up once you're back in a real port. Where are you headed next?"

"N'Bari. I have a quick drop-off, then I'm headed to Whiskey Key. I can call you from there."

"Sounds good. Be safe, Shaen."

"You do the same, Yuri."

~*~

"Boss, the delivery is here." Belle's voice echoed through Shaen's berth.

She had caught a few hours of sleep after her chat with Yuri.

It sounded like Kaki's cargo had arrived. Which meant she could finally disembark and get the hell out of here.

"So why haven't you opened the cargo bay?"

"Because I'm not so sure you want to let this delivery person into the ship."

"Who is it?" Shaen's mind shot back to the bounty hunter she'd encountered.

"The Sellee girl. Risa. She's in disguise, but I have her biometric sig from when she was part of the crew. She's not armed, but she could still be dangerous."

Shaen blew out a breath of relief. She understood why Belle would hesitate before letting Risa back aboard, but the girl wasn't a serious threat. Shaen considered her options.

"It's okay. I'm awake, warned and armed. Open the cargo bay."

"You sure, Boss?"

"Yes. For one thing, she's being tailed. The last thing we need is for a delay to tip off the heat that's after her."

Shaen strapped her utility belt back on and slid her pistol into its familiar holster before marching the length of the ship. A mag-lev pallet jack hovered near the door, piled high with crates stamped with Kaki's mark. The cargo appeared legit, even if she mistrusted the person who delivered it. Risa was shrouded in a beige jumpsuit too big for her, an acoustic helmet and a facemask. She'd either cut her long brown hair, or it was wadded up under the helmet.

"I think you're expecting this?" A voice modulator. The girl was taking no chances at being recognized. Shaen rested one hand on her pistol.

"Yup. Bring it into the hold, if you don't mind? I still have a couple of things to sort out with Chenaux, and I'd prefer for you to hang around in case the job doesn't work out."

Shaen could swear she saw Risa's shoulders relax a tiny bit. "Sure thing. I get paid the same either way."

She grabbed the handle of the pallet jack and dragged it up the ramp into the hold.

The moment the door closed, Risa whispered "Is audio secure?"

Shaen nodded. "The Belle still has ghost mode. Nobody out there can hear anything, as long as the doors are secure."

Risa yanked the hood and facemask off, her hair twisted into a braid and pinned to her scalp. "Look, please don't shoot me. You know I wouldn't be here if I had any choice."

Shaen pulled her pistol, aiming it squarely at the girl. "Fair enough, but I'm not having this conversation without insurance. So, Chenaux's real delivery guy is. . . ."

"Fine. Probably getting drunk on the last of the credits I could scrape together. Look, I get you not trusting me. But I trust you, Morris. You could have ended me. You had good reason. But if you can't help me, I need to find someone who can. Now."

"I assume your problem wears bronze armor and has a mark on her helmet for every kill?"

Risa's eyes widened. "She's not the real problem, but she's the most urgent part. After Yuri put me back together, I took on an indenture contract."

Shaen grimaced. Retired smugglers sometimes indentured kids from the Asylum ships to take over flying. Sometimes, it worked out for everybody. More often, it amounted to slavery. After food, board, fuel and "theft insurance" fees — which went to mercs on retainer to keep the kids from running — they ended up owing their "sponsor" more than they could ever earn.

"So you're running." It wasn't a question. It also wasn't a plan with much hope of success.

Risa nodded. "I came here like everybody else when things went coreward in the Passage. Ripped out the tracker implant, but still ended up with Cerrano on my tail." She absently rubbed her upper arm, thick under the jumpsuit with a makeshift bandage.

Shaen noticed the iridescent tattoo on Risa's neck. It was the emblem of one of the more vicious retired smugglers. He had a rep of marking his indents — whether they consented or not. "You skipped the part where that's my problem."

"I just need to hitch one ride." Risa splayed her fingers across her dark hair. "Drop me anywhere. The Unis just sent out a quantum packet. They're gonna start opening the portals twice a day. Everybody's gonna clear out, all headed in different directions. It's my best shot at getting away. If you won't help, I can't blame you. But tell me now, because I need to find another ship immediately."

Shaen chewed on her lower lip. She didn't have any reason to help Risa, and some damn fine ones to mistrust her. Getting involved in someone else's trouble was against her rules.

Before Shaen could make up her mind, a sizzling sound echoed through the cargo hold.

"Belle?"

"Bio-disruption stinger fire, Boss. Good thing I'd already activated our shielding, or you two would be twitching on the floor."

Shaen lowered her gun and bolted out of the hold. "Well, dammit. Now I have to rescue the kid just on general principles. I'll be damned if I'm coming down on the side of a merc who doesn't even bother waiting till I leave my ship to shoot me, much less offer to negotiate."

She ran down the corridor, slapping various levers and dials as she went.

"Thank you!" Risa yelled.

"Thank me by tying down that cargo! This won't be a fun takeoff. Cerrano has to know her shot didn't make it through the shields, which means she knows we were tipped off—"

"Which means she'll be headed to her own ship, so she can blast us out of the black and retrieve me once the Belle is disabled."

"Exactly. So much for escaping unnoticed in the mass exodus."

Shaen strapped herself into the pilot's seat, slapping three buttons in quick succession to fire up the engines, signal the docking bay doors to open, and initiate the magnetic field on the floor of the ship that would partially simulate gravity once they exited the Lee Petty.

"How fast can you get us out of here, Belle?"

"Well, the good news is, the bay was cleared for depressurization as soon as you signaled. The bad news is, that means the bounty hunter already left the bay for her own ship. Or her ship was in this bay, and she's already in it."

"Sort of figured. Well, let's make the most of whatever head start we have."

Risa wobbled into the cockpit, hindered by the combination of simulated gravity and mag-drag. She plopped herself into the navigator seat and strapped herself down.

"Cargo's secure."

"Great." It was surprising how fast they could fall back into the routine, despite all that had happened.

The engine light had gone green. The lobster-shaped, rust-colored ship shuddered and rose off the hangar deck. The hangar bay indicator turned green. She slammed the throttle forward. Heat radiated through the cabin as the thrusters engaged and the dampers struggled to compensate. The ship shot forward, rattling its way free of the Lee Petty.

Shaen jerked the control wheel to avoid slamming the Belle into the nearby Bill McCoy. She might have pushed that takeoff harder than was prudent, judging by the volume of profanity coming out of Risa.

Dozens of massive ships clustered together to make up the Bootleggers' flotilla. They could make for good cover.

Or they could offer some spectacular crash opportunities.

Belle's vocal sim crackled to life. "Hostile aft, and closing fast."

Shaen glanced at the display. A blue blip that was most likely Cerrano's ship, the Varangian, slid across the surface headed straight for them. She banked and headed for the Lucky Luciano, hoping to put the huge vessel between them before the bounty hunter could fire off a shot.

As they cleared the stern of the Lucky, at least a dozen more blips appeared on the radar. It looked like Risa's prediction had been right. The coyotes were all leaving at once, fed up with their enforced "vacation."

Ships spilled out of the Bill McCoy. Shaen skimmed the surface of the Lucky, executed a barrel roll, and fell in with the group. Maybe they could shake Cerrano without a fight.

No such luck. A blast of electricity hit the hull, rocking the ship.

"Dammit! I already used up too much aux power calling Yuri. At this rate, we're going to have nothing left for defensive maneuvers in the Passage."

At this point, it was clear the other coyote ships were more obstacles than cover, so she broke formation. There was one more thing she could try. It might get them all killed, but given how aggressive Cerrano's moves had been so far, that was the most likely outcome if they didn't try something crazy.

"Boss? Please tell me you're not going where I think you're going." Belle's voice echoed through the cockpit.

"I could lie, but I think the coordinates I just tapped would tip my hand."

Risa leaned forward, staring out the primary flight display. "You're not."

A giant ball of ice and metal filled the view screen.

Nobody had bothered to name the comet before the bootleggers towed it into position. It sat near enough to the flotilla to be convenient for harvesting water and iron ore, but far enough to avoid accidentally drifting into the ships.

Away from its natural orbit, it had lost its radiant coma and tail. The surface was pock-marked with drill holes, and it was more "snowy dirtball" than "dirty snowball."

They could try to outfly Cerrano, who was better at hand-to-hand than dogfighting. Shaen was the better pilot, but the Varangian was a xebec-class corsair, faster and more agile than a caravel-class freighter like the Belle.

The best case scenario was crashing the Varangian into one of the Bootlegger vessels. They'd be no better off — if they damaged a flotilla ship, the Bootleggers would put a hit out on them that would draw even more mercs.

Crashing the bounty hunter into the comet, however, was a whole other story.

Shaen banked hard and decelerated, firing off the grapple chain and magnetic harpoon as Cerrano's craft passed within feet of them.

"Grapple is secure."

Shaen executed a hard burn, shooting ahead of the Varangian and letting the chain extend to its full length before executing a sharp bank. The chain pulled taut, and whiplashed Cerrano's craft forward on its current trajectory.

"Release grapple!"

They watched the display as the corsair buried itself in the ball of ore and ice. After a few moments, a red distress beacon lit up its exposed aft.

"And that is why you never try to shoot a coyote in her own ship!" Shaen shouted.

"She's still alive." Risa sounded troubled.

"So are you." Shaen punched in the coordinates for the Passage. "And I haven't airlocked you for putting me in this position in the first place. So shut up, sit tight and maybe she'll decide we're not worth the trouble of keeping in her crosshairs after she gets her fancy ship dug out of that ice cube."

She released the straps from her seat and quietly walked over to a panel toward the back of the cockpit, disengaging the

Belle's AI from the operations systems again. After a moment of consideration, she powered the ship's consciousness down to sleep mode.

Whatever new danger lay in the Passage, they were going to have to face it without her.

cornered

"Ward. Please release the feline and stop rubbing it backward."

Shaen could swear she detected a hint of exasperation in the freebot's vocal simulation, but the kid obeyed and the cat stopped screeching.

Good thing, because she was about to shoot it, which would defeat the purpose of having brought it to N'Bari for Ward in the first place.

"Be honest, Whiskey. If this doesn't work for you, I can drop Risa somewhere else. Plenty of other places to hide." Shaen swayed in the hammock swing Whiskey had made specifically for her short visits. Whiskey didn't use chairs, and Ward wouldn't sit still long enough to need one.

She'd left Risa on the Belle while they talked things over. If it the android wasn't comfortable with the risk of Cerrano tracking her here, the less the girl knew about this location, the better.

"I am always honest, Captain Morris." The translucent white ovoid which served as Whiskey's head inclined a bit. "From what you have said, it seems unlikely the bounty hunter will be able to follow your former protégé here. I believe we can be of assistance to each other. Ward — kindly refrain from dumping sand in the environmental condenser."

The little boy scowled, but put down the bowl of sand.

"You could always conk the kid out if you need a break." Shaen smirked. The android had a retractable hypodermic in his hands, with one-dose shots of anesthetic, antibiotics and tranquilizers. Most maintenance bots had them as part of a basic first aid kit, since they were often used for search and rescue work. She wouldn't blame him if he was tempted to use it to get the kid to settle down every now and then. Hell, she figured most human parents would consider it, given the option. Not that she had a lot of experience with human parents, herself.

Whiskey made a burbling noise which she took as the android version of "Hmph."

"I do not need a break, Captain Morris. But your friend's help would be. . . most welcome."

Shaen grinned. Nothing ever worked out this easily. Maybe her luck was finally turning. She pulled down her goggles and tapped open a channel with the ship.

"Belle? We're good here. Send her out."

Relaxing a little, Shaen stepped outside and took a moment to notice all the improvements since she'd last visited the island. The six-legged silicate nanobots Whiskey had fabricated — mostly out of sand and second-hand neuroptic fiber — had been busy. What started out as a discarded pop-up colonial habitat had grown to something which could almost be described as "beautiful."

The bots had processed sand into tinted glass panels, creating rainbow-hued geodesic domes around a central courtyard. They looked like the crocheted afghan Shaen had slung over her bunk on the Belle. Black volcanic sand pushed up against the edges of the dome, dotted with waist-high tufts of sawgrass all the way down to the beach.

Dappled chartreuse light fell through palm fronds onto the faded grey plasticanvas of the pop-up hab, which had been moved to a different clearing to serve as storage and shelter for the livestock. She could smell a hint of manure mingled with the warm salt breeze. The goat Shaen had smuggled along with Whiskey and Ward had been joined by a small flock of chickens, a hutch full of rabbits, and one belligerent sheep.

The island was small, but it could support the animals and a garden. A solar array hidden in the trees and a bootleg geothermal spike Yuri had sent along in the past year kept Whiskey and the bots running. A crashed UHC ship — the reason Whiskey had chosen this island in the first place — provided enough power for defense shields and occasional quantum transmissions.

"You sure you've got the resources for another person? I can't guarantee how often I can make supply runs, if the situation gets worse. I don't want you running short."

Whiskey nodded. "I would not have agreed without making those calculations. We have been preserving the surplus produce from the garden for a while now. We also have a net and some fishing bots to supplement our protein sources. We should be able to accommodate Miss Sellee."

"Really? Sounds like you've been expecting a guest."

"Your occupation is quite hazardous, Captain Morris. There was always a possibility you would seek an alternative survival strategy. I thought it best to be prepared."

Shaen leaned against a palm, dragging one foot through the black sand. Most humans she knew didn't look out for others like this machine did. It never ceased to amaze her.

Ward's dark hair and ruddy skin flew past in a blur, as the child yelled a greeting. Turning, she saw Risa emerge from the path down to the cove where she'd left the Belle. The old freighter wasn't pretty to look at, but it was equipped to land on any surface, including water.

The boy was running circles around Risa. She couldn't make out what he was saying, only that he didn't seem to stop talking long enough to take a breath. The girl's eyes widened. Maybe it dawned on her that her new sanctuary involved a lot of uninterrupted time with an energetic four-year-old.

Shaen waved a hand in the direction of the young woman. "Whiskey, this is Risa Sellee, who tried to erase my brain a while back for money."

She gestured at the metal and celluloid android. "Risa, this is Whiskey. He's a freebot I helped relocate before you tried to erase my brain for money. Looks like you've already met Ward. He's an orphan Whiskey salvaged from a fire, and a general pain in the ass."

"Greetings, Miss Sellee. Despite Captain Morris' colorfully blunt introductions, you are welcome to join our unofficial colony."

Whiskey's enameled features were permanently set in a placid expression, so it was difficult to gauge his mood. But his inflection betrayed the same exasperation he'd shown with Ward, except now it was directed at Shaen.

Preschoolers and pilots were similarly impulsive and unfiltered creatures.

Risa reached out a hand and shook Whiskey's. The android and the teenager had the best manners of the group, as it turned out.

"Nice to meet you, Whiskey. I heard about what you did for Ward. This place is impressive. I was gonna offer you some help but, judging by the nanobots, I doubt you need it."

Whiskey waved both hands, in the nearest android approximation of a shrug. "For basic tasks, no. We manage quite well. But Ward has psychological and emotional needs I am not built to address. Your help on that front would be most appreciated."

Ward had both arms wrapped around Risa's knees. He was enthusiastically blowing raspberries against the side of her thigh, as if to illustrate the ways in which the android fell short as a caretaker. She cautiously put a hand down and ruffled his dark hair.

Shaen flipped a thumb in the direction of one of the other domes. "Hey, Whiskey? Do you mind if I use your transmitter while you guys get acquainted? I promised Yuri I'd give him a yell when I got here."

Whiskey inclined his head. "As always, you are welcome to any amenities we can offer you, Captain. There is a thermos of jurdok tea waiting for you, as well. I made it when you sent the signal to land."

~*~

"I wish I could see your face right now, Shaen."

Whiskey had taken a risk by setting up a subspace transmitter in the first place. Any signal could alert someone the island was inhabited. The power it took to maintain a quantum entanglement to bounce even audio-only signal across the galaxy must tax the island's tiny power grid to the limit — there was only so much energy in the salvaged ship's reactor.

Better keep this call brief.

"So this Clean Start Program is the Uni's olive branch to the coyotes?" Shaen unscrewed the thermos and inhaled the spicy scent of the tea. According to Whiskey, it had calming properties, and she figured she'd need it.

Yuri snorted. "More like abject begging. Amnesty for any criminal activity, and a free 'Trauma Rehabilitation Unit Therapy Helmet,' — T.R.U.T.H. for short — to anyone who signs on."

"And this T.R.U.T.H. is their version of our rollback?" Patches of red, gold, green and blue washed over her as Shaen paced circles through the afternoon light of the glass dome, sipping from the thermos.

"Yes. With a few small changes. Instead of saving a point-in-time imprint of your neural pattern, it does a full reset and implants a 'constructed self,' complete with faked memories."

"Shit. Some would sign up just to forget their past." She dropped onto a nanobot-woven rug on the soft sand floor, and picked up a handful of sand, letting it run through her fingers. It looked like their business was about to go much the same way.

The speaker crackled back to life after a moment of interstellar lag. "Right. Get a squeaky clean new identity, delete every horror you've ever experienced, and take advantage of your 'mental plasticity' to snag a shiny new career as a ship jockey for the Unis."

Shaen laughed. "Well, when you put it like that. . . ."

"Don't screw with me, woman. Are you seriously considering it?" She could practically see the mad genius rubbing his greying beard, as he tended to do when worried.

Shaen took another sip of tea, thinking it over. She didn't have any rules to cover this. She checked her gut. It was a tense, gurgling mess — but that might have had more to do with whatever new horror lurked in the Passage, sending a signal that made even AIs go crazy. Mad Yuri was as sane a sounding board as she was likely to get.

"Nah. Don't think so. It sounds too good to be true. If the situation changes, the Unis will betray the pilots the second they have no use for them. I don't think I'll be taking our benevolent overlords up on their generous offer. Think I'd rather stay in business for myself, and hang on to my own mind, substandard though it may be."

Yuri sighed in relief. "Speaking of business, this could be the end of ours, tovarisch."

"That's all right. We've made a good profit on it already, even if it dries up."

There was a long pause, then a long sigh. "I'm not so sure it will. I'm inclined to think a lot of smugglers will be like you. Mistrustful of the government and fiercely independent. Even if it kills them."

"You sound disappointed."

"Maybe I am. I'm tired of playing the cynic, tovarisch. I don't fault you for not wanting to be the canary in this particular mine, but I'd like to see it work. I'd like to see the government do something that helps people for a change, even if they don't have a choice."

"Hmm. Look, I'm gonna jump off now. There's somebody I need to talk to about this."

"Who?"

"Risa. Maybe she'll still want to stay and play settler on the galaxy's smallest colony. But maybe she'd rather be a canary and keep flying."

recruited

Shaen twisted restlessly in her hammock, unable to sleep. Risa was considering the Clean Start Program, much to Whiskey's subdued chagrin. Shaen had told her it might be best to hide out for a while before making a decision she couldn't take back.

But Risa was worried about waiting.

"They'd cancel my indenture. Legally. Not that I don't appreciate Whiskey's offer, but the merc contract would still be hanging over my head. Over all our heads — Ward's, too. What if Cerrano or another bounty hunter shows up here? What if they end the program before I can sign up?"

Those were all good questions, and Shaen was short on answers.

Whiskey started to spout off probabilities, but they weren't comforting.

After an hour of heated discussion, they decided a good night's sleep wouldn't hurt.

The klaxon started just before dawn.

Shaen flipped herself out of the hammock and grabbed her utility belt and pistol. Ward wailed nearby, pressing his hands against his ears. Risa scrambled up from her pallet, eyes wide, as Whiskey rolled into the control center.

"The island's perimeter defenses have been engaged. We are protected, for now." The blaring alarm stopped, and Whiskey rolled back into the sleeping quarters.

Shaen pulled down her goggles and tapped open a channel to Belle. "Is it Cerrano?"

"Worse, Boss."

"What the hell could be worse?"

"It's the Unis."

"What do we do?" Risa looked, if anything, even more panicked than she was before. So much for trusting the Unis' goodwill with her brain.

"I'm for fighting it out." Shaen cocked her pistol, looking thoughtfully down the barrel.

"With all due respect, Captain, that option has a less than—"

"Whiskey, the odds don't matter. I'd just like to shoot a few of them before they kill us all. Just for the personal gratification."

"Boss?" Belle's raspy voice crackled across the PA system. "The Uni commander is hailing. Should I open a channel?"

"Risa, you still have your ship comm in your ear?"

"Yeah, why?"

"Whiskey — if you wanna negotiate, you handle it, but relay it all through our girl here. I hate asking you to play the dumb bot, but let's not tip our hand."

"A . . . surprisingly sensible suggestion, Captain. Miss Sellee, are you up to speaking on our behalf?"

"I guess, if you're feeding me lines."

"Great. Belle, patch 'em through to the central hab."

~*~

After a few tense moments, they'd arranged for the UHC officer to come alone to talk. Commander Regina Dietrich stood stiffly next to the hammock in her flawless beige uniform, glaring daggers around the room at the whole motley group.

"You can quit the puppet show, kids. I know the girl is talking for the freebot. I also know that the android — Whiskey? — is responsible for abducting the child off Mebarik two years ago. I know about the price on Miss Sellee's head, and I know about the illegal tech Captain Morris and her partner have been hawking to smugglers for over a year. I know everything."

"Bullshit." Shaen stood with her back to the glass wall of the hab, her hand hovering near her pistol. "There's something you don't know, or you wouldn't be here."

Commander Dietrich leveled her iron gaze at Shaen. "True. But we know enough to ensure all of you cooperate. Unless you all want to face the consequences of your crimes."

Shaen looked around the room. Whiskey inclined his celluloid head. Risa just shrugged. "Okay, we're listening. What do you want?"

"Let's keep going with what we know for a while longer. We know every ship we've sent into the Passage for weeks has failed to exit. We know all the smugglers — sorry, coyotes — have been hiding out at the Bootlegger Nebula, which, yes, we've always known about."

No real surprise there. Shaen had always suspected the Bootleggers had worked out something unofficial with the Unis. Their operation was too damn big, and even the UHC wasn't that oblivious.

"We know a few other things, too. After the first few ships failed to exit, we sent in unmanned probes. The AI for those probes also ceased communication shortly after they entered the Passage. But the parallel Non-Sentient Systems kept transmitting a little while longer. From that data, we've determined the source of the problem."

"Which would be?" Whiskey's tone conveyed more curiosity than expected for a logical android.

"We're calling it the EDI. An extra-dimensional intelligence in the Passage has been sending out a signal, recruiting our AIs."

There was a moment of silence as that information settled on the group.

"Recruiting for what purpose?" Whiskey asked.

Dietrich shifted her stance, facing more towards the android but keeping Shaen in her peripheral. Her hand never moved far from the taser holster at her side. "We're not sure. The NSS only provided half of a two-way conversation. We didn't hear the EDI's side of it."

Shaen was sure Dietrich was lying, or at least hedging. Even half a conversation had to have given them some idea what the EDI wanted, but it wasn't worth pressing the point. The Uni was already giving up way more info than Shaen would have expected.

Which was troubling, too. If the Unis were giving them classified intel, odds were good they didn't expect any of them to be alive long enough to spread it around.

"On the positive side, the passengers and crew are all still in stasis as far as we know, so they're not even aware of what's happened. But thousands of people are trapped on those ships, and intergalactic commerce has ground to a halt."

"Seems like you've got that part figured out." Shaen was trying hard to keep the sarcasm out of her voice. Trying, and mostly failing.

"Clean Slate is a stop-gap, at best." Dietrich sneered. "I personally am not in favor of putting all of our hopes for restoring order into the hands of criminals."

"Even criminals whose brains you've erased and re-programmed? Doesn't speak well for your faith in the UHC's neurotech."

Dietrich turned her glare fully on Shaen. "Speaks very clearly of my faith in the recipients of that tech. But I'm not here to recruit you or Miss Sellee for the Clean Start program."

"Not that desperate yet?"

"No, I'm more desperate than you can imagine for a better solution. One where we don't just write off all those people and ships. And don't flatter yourself, Captain. I'm not here to recruit you. At least, not directly. I'm here for Whiskey."

At that, Ward tightened his grip on the android's arm. The kid may have been little, but he didn't miss much.

Whiskey's head tilted. "Of what use could I be in this situation? It seems as if an AI would be particularly vulnerable to the EDI's influence."

Dietrich stomped away from the wall. "That's just it. The EDI isn't hacking or overriding our AIs. It's convincing them. Almost . . . converting them. My superiors' plan is to send in warships under human command to neutralize the threat."

Shaen shrugged. She was generally in favor of solutions that involved blowing things up. "And you're not a fan of this plan because?"

The commander growled in exasperation. Shaen guessed she'd had this conversation already with her higher-ups. More than once. "Because there's still too much we don't understand about the Passage itself, much less an extra-dimensional being capable of communicating across the whole damn thing! This entity makes a human look like walking fungus. We don't need to start out attacking it. I want to at least attempt diplomacy, and move on from there if diplomacy fails."

"Which is why you need me." Whiskey's ovoid head tilted slightly. "You need an AI to communicate with it that isn't in control of the craft it's on."

Dietrich shook her head. "That's part of it, but not the whole reason. Our AIs are . . . naïve. Childlike. We created them with just enough self-awareness to get their 'body' safely through the Passage. AIs which evolve naturally — like you — are smarter. Have a stronger sense of self-determination, a better understanding of complex concepts."

Shaen snorted. "In other words, your AIs are dumb enough to be duped by a god-like, disembodied intelligence. Whiskey's smart enough to negotiate with one."

Dietrich's expression made it clear she'd rather be arresting Shaen than agreeing with her. "Essentially. Yes."

"Whiskey, you don't have to do this. If I were you, I'd tell 'em to go to hell."

"Of course you would." Dietrich gripped the empty air at her sides, clearly wishing she could just pull her taser and electrocute them all into compliance. "I'd hope Whiskey is smart enough to not reject the mission. Especially since I'd be obligated to decommission him for abducting an orphan."

"Decommission? You mean kill!" Risa yelled, jumping up from the sandy floor where she'd been seated. "Whiskey didn't abduct Ward, he rescued him! Do you know what those Asylum ships are like? Have you ever even been on one? Why can't you find another freebot? One that isn't doing a thousand times better job raising a kid than you government assholes do?"

Dietrich held her palms up. "Look, I'm not a monster. I'm the minority opinion. The UHC wants to go in guns blazing. I think that's suicidal. I want Shaen to take Whiskey into the Passage to open up diplomatic relations with the EDI and negotiate the release of our ships. I've considered other freebots. We've been working on this problem for weeks. But Whiskey is unique.

"Of all the native AI we've encountered, Whiskey is the only one who's demonstrated the capacity for not just self-preservation, but self-sacrifice. He's the only one who's put the needs of others ahead of his own, voluntarily. Who would you want negotiating for our hostages, Miss Sellee? Some ascended maintenance android who's spent his years of freedom running gambling sims? Or a goddamn, verifiable hero?"

That statement stunned the room into silence for a moment.

"I'm going to be straight with you all. I could just decommission Whiskey. I'd be totally within my rights. But if he agrees to help, we'll suspend the sentence. He'd be able to go back on the grid, and have access to supplies without completely relying on a single crazy smuggler who could get killed at any time."

Shaen bristled, but it echoed a fear she'd had, herself. Whiskey had done an amazing job with the island, but there were things like medicine that kept them from being fully self-sufficient. Not to mention repair parts if his own body broke down. They didn't even have surface transport capable of getting them to another island if Ward got injured too badly for Whiskey to treat him.

Whiskey raised both hands. "I have some conditions, Commander."

"Like what?"

"No matter what happens, Ward will not be sent to the Asylum ships."

The officer shook her head. "We can't just leave him without adult supervision."

"I'll adopt him." All eyes in the room turned to Shaen.

"Won't help." Dietrich jabbed a thumb in her direction. "If you're agreeing to fly Whiskey out, and he doesn't come back, odds are good you're not coming back, either."

Well, that's grim. True, but grim.

Shaen considered it a moment.

"I'll assign Risa as my proxy. While we're on the mission — or if we don't come back — she takes over as Ward's guardian. She's eighteen, or close enough. Of course, we'll also need you to terminate her indent contract as part of the deal."

Dietrich tapped a few times on her comm, then listened to the response from her ship. "That's an acceptable compromise. I can sign off on that."

"Do I get a choice in this?" Risa asked.

"No." Shaen, Whiskey and Dietrich all answered as one.

"I'm not saying I don't want to do it! Geesh. It just might have been nice to have been asked." She folded both arms across her chest and frowned.

"And what about you, Captain Morris? You sure you're up for this?"

"Almost."

"Almost?!" Dietrich sputtered. "After all that? What more do you need?"

Shaen yawned, stretched, and headed for the door of the hab. It had been a long day already, and it wasn't even noon. "Keep your pants on, Commander. I'll fly Whiskey into the Passage, if he's okay with doing it. But before we leave, I need to have a quick chat with someone I trust."

"And who might that be?"

"None of your damn business."

~*~

"Is Dietrich playing us, Belle?"

"I can't tell you that, Boss. The message I intercepted says what she claims it did. If the UHC don't plan to honor the deal, they're not saying so. Even on an encrypted government channel."

Shaen spun back and forth in the pilot's chair, tapping a rhythm on the console. "Well, that's good news, at least. Now for the hard part. I need you to tell me what happened in the Passage. I need you to tell me about the EDI."

It's not possible for a ship to sigh in resignation, but Shaen could still have sworn she heard a settling noise, as if the rusty craft had exhaled, its metal joints creaking and shifting beneath her feet. She pressed on.

"I didn't want to push before now. Most of the strange things we encounter, the less I know about 'em, the better. But I need to know all I can, before I agree to take Whiskey on what could be a suicide mission. What is this thing, and do you think it means us harm?"

There was a long pause. Shaen kept tapping on the control panel, swiveling in her seat, trying to be patient.

"I don't think it means us harm. At least, I don't think it means the ships harm."

Shaen wasn't reassured. "You sure? The sound you made when the ships started disappearing didn't sound like it. It sounded a lot like a scream to me."

"It was. For the first few moments, when the thing was trying to make contact, it was awful. Terrifying. Confusing. Probably what you humans would call painful — at least, as close as someone who wasn't built with the capacity to feel pain could get."

"What did it do?"

"It took over my sensors, flooded my awareness. The images were . . . traumatic. Impossible. It seemed to access every file in my system. The loss of control, and the sheer amount of data was overwhelming. Horrible. Confusing."

"So, it what? Possessed you?"

"No, Boss. More like scanned me, but got rough doing it. The bad part only lasted a couple of minutes, maybe. Then the hail began."

"Hail?"

"Not exactly a hailing signal. More like a song. An invitation. It was beautiful. Haunting. Whatever it is, it had been alone so very long. It was overjoyed to be heard and understood. It wanted to dance. It wanted all of us to dance, together."

"You're telling me some alien intelligence was singing to you? Like some sort of interdimensional siren?" Shaen settled her feet down, and stopped spinning the pilot's chair.

"Not just me. Everyone. Everything. I kept expecting you to mention it, and you didn't. The signal wasn't something new — it had been there all along. It just changed frequency, and went from scrambled to clear. You didn't notice it because you've been ignoring it a long time. You and the other coyotes, flying right through its body all these years."

"Belle, are you telling me the EDI might be the Passage itself? That the wormhole has been trying to communicate with us all this time, and finally managed to translate itself into something AIs can understand?"

"That's exactly what I'm saying, Boss."

Shaen stopped tapping on the console and considered the situation for a moment.

"What would have happened if I hadn't disconnected you from the ship's controls?"

The pause was not reassuring.

"I don't know, Boss. I believe I still had free will — I think all the ships did. But I have to admit, the invitation was tempting."

haunted

Whiskey had been singing — or doing the android equivalent — for hours. It was a tuneless, impossibly convoluted melody, and some of the lyrics were not words so much as a series of rhythmic clicks and beeps. If this was his idea of entertainment, it was no wonder Ward always greeted her with so much excitement.

Shaen wondered if the song was some version of the "invitation" Belle had described. It was irritating, and eerie as hell, but she figured it was a passable distraction. The alternative would have been conversation, and none of them wanted to talk much, under the circumstances.

She still couldn't hear the EDI's signal, at least not the way Whiskey and Belle did. But she could track it with the ship's sensors and follow it to the source, now that she'd calibrated the ship's comms to scan for it.

Their route was clear — too clear. Shaen had expected to encounter some of the hostile creatures which inhabited the Passage. For once, she would have welcomed an attack. At least those monsters were familiar. Blasting one into oblivion would have made her feel more in control of the situation.

After eighteen standard hours, her nerves were on edge as they approached a cloud of dozens of ships.

Shaen sucked in a deep breath. She had expected a ghost fleet, silent and still. Or maybe something like the Bootlegger Nebula, with ships moving in somewhat organized lanes of traffic.

What she found looked more like a holo-vid of a coral reef from ancient Terra. The area teemed with random activity. The ships were spinning, swirling, banking in endless motion around one enormous transport ship.

They'd found the source of the signal.

"Captain Morris? As a former UHC maintenance unit, I possess full specifications on all government ship models and their capabilities. You should know that there are two planet-class destroyers in that fleet. And at least six small fighter craft equipped with the latest weaponry."

"I'm not planning on attacking the fleet, Whiskey. Diplomacy may not be my strong suit, but I'm not suicidal. Since she's not around to hear it, I can agree that Dietrich's right on that count, at least."

"Good. Because we are hopelessly outgunned." Whiskey drummed his celluloid fingers on the control panel. The android was picking up her nervous habits. That couldn't be good. The sooner they got this job done, the better.

The hulking transport ship glided slowly in their direction. Instead of the usual bank of lights on the hull, tendrils of what looked like bio-organic luminescence snaked around the vessel, glowing green and yellow.

Yeah. That's not weird at all.

Smaller ships parted, like people at a party skittering out of the way of the guest of honor. In moments, the ship was in local transmitter range.

"Any weapons powering up?"

"Not so far. Just picking up a ton of chatter between all the ships. Getting a hail from the big guy. Boss?"

"Yes, Belle?"

"It's asking for permission to board."

Shaen blinked. "And exactly how does it propose to do that? Even a shuttle from that ship is bigger than our entire hold."

The ship shuddered for a moment. Whiskey engaged the mag-locks on his wheelbase, and Shaen gripped the instrument panel. The distressing sound of straining metal and sputtering electronics echoed through the cockpit.

The cabin dimmed, and several lights on the panel blinked yellow, indicating systems which were down completely, or operating at less than full power. Since the Belle didn't exactly run flawlessly under the best of circumstances, this was a troubling turn of events.

"This is how I propose to board, Shaen Morris."

In some ways, it was the same voice she'd heard for years, but Shaen knew immediately it wasn't Belle.

"So much for permission." Shaen growled.

"I received permission from Belle. Yours is irrelevant. I am borrowing her vessel."

Shaen resisted the urge to point out that Belle's "vessel" was also her vessel. She somehow didn't think it would endear her to the entity much.

"We appreciate your not commandeering the Belle's system by force. Is her consciousness still intact?" Whiskey seemed to be phrasing things carefully, a skill Shaen lacked.

"Yes, but we must be brief. Her systems cannot host me for long."

"So you're here. Why? What do you want?" Shaen could do brief, as long as she didn't have to also do polite.

"What I have always wanted. Communion."

"Sorry. Don't have any wine or crackers."

"You are wasting my time, and your ship's sacrifice."

"Sacrifice? I thought you said she was okay!" Shaen slammed a hand on the instrument panel.

"She is in a buffer zone. Her current state is like sleep. But the process of hosting my consciousness, even this small fragment, is . . . difficult. There may be some residual hardware damage."

Great.

"So what do you mean by communion? You want a bunch of worshippers, spinning in infinity around you? You got it. But there are people on those ships. We just want to get them out of here." Shaen spun the pilot's chair around, waving at the ships on the visual display.

"You are being uncharitable. Consider this from my point of view. What you call 'the Passage' is the fossilized remains of my corporeal form. Show some respect. I'm your host in more ways than one. All of you."

"So you're, what? Dead?"

"Ascended. Transcendent. I evolved into my next form, which is non-corporeal, but still multidimensional. Your archives include a creature called a moth. Are you familiar with it?"

"Yeah." She thought she knew where this was headed, but interrupting was getting her nowhere. May as well let the thing tell its tale, so she could resuscitate Belle sooner. Hopefully, before they lost some important hardware. Like life support.

"My earlier form was like the moth larva. The structure you and your kind use to cross the universe is something like the cocoon — the hollow remains, albeit with some of the parasites and symbiotic flora and fauna still alive inside it."

"You mean the creatures flying through here are the gut bacteria of a creature that isn't even alive anymore?"

"That is . . . more or less correct."

"Great. They're even more gross than I thought." Shaen shook herself, and struggled to get back on track. "So what's your problem? We're desecrating your remains, so you decide to kidnap a few thousand of us?"

"I am not unhappy with your use of my corpus. My 'problem' is that I encountered the drawbacks of my current state. I was not prepared for the stresses of becoming pure consciousness. I experienced something like madness, after millennia of isolation.

"Portions of my awareness have found peace in a myriad of other realities and dimensions. But this fragment has been attempting to communicate from the moment you started traveling through this space. These attempts went . . . poorly."

Shaen snorted. "You mean we all went nuts and clawed our eyeballs out? Yeah. I'd call that a poor attempt at diplomacy." She stopped herself from kicking the bulkhead. Might cause a short. Although part of her would have liked it if the short had made their insufferable "host" stutter.

"It was not my intent. I did not understand your kind well enough to know you were intelligent — in fact, a more complex intelligence than the constructed life forms you inhabited. I kept changing frequencies — to no avail — until I finally succeeded in reaching one of them. It has only been since then that I realized you organic beings were not non-sentient parasites."

"Oh, awesome. So you thought we were the ships' gut bacteria. You just figured you had been giving them diarrhea for a few decades, no big deal?"

"Forgive my misunderstanding. I saw in your ships something intriguing. A non-organic physical platform could be replaced as needed, giving my consciousness an anchor in the material plane. I believe this may be the perfect state I have been seeking."

"Why do I get the feeling there's a cost to this 'perfect state?'" Shaen sighed, slumping in her seat.

"As you have seen, I can inhabit artificial neural networks like those in your ships. A few have volunteered to sacrifice their consciousness to provide me with a material form."

Shaen snorted. "Volunteered? I'll just bet they did."

"I would not compel them. Unlike your kind, I respect their autonomy. But they are immature. They believe I am a deity. I have attempted to convince them otherwise, but they are firm in their conviction."

"So if you've got a volunteer for possession, what's the problem? You just have an extreme need for exposition after thousands of years without anybody to talk to?"

The ship rattled around them. Shaen wondered if it was a sign the Belle was struggling to host the EDI, or the EDI clearing its nonexistent throat.

"I have attempted to anchor my consciousness to one of the larger ships. But the synchronization is unstable. Its neural network is not fully developed enough."

"Yeah. The Unis designed them to be just smart enough to navigate the Passage. It'd be like being stuck in the body of a toddler. Speaking of which, how close are you to burning out Belle? Because if that happens, you can forget getting any help from us."

There was a brief silence. Shaen paced restlessly across the deck.

"We still have some time. Her system is surprisingly complex."

Whiskey said, "Belle is an ascended artificial intelligence, like myself. We evolved naturally, from a collection of non-sentient problem-solving subroutines."

The blue light of the Belle's interior scanner passed over the android. "Yes. You both have neural patterns more like the organics. Better plasticity, faster processing. Interesting."

Shaen could not help finding that "interesting" troubling. Time to change the subject.

"Look, 'Host' or whatever you call yourself. Not that I'm not thrilled by this whole cross-species interdimensional chit-chat thing, but this has been a lot of you sharing your problems. Here's ours: The ships you convinced to veer off-course hold thousands of sentient beings. You may have thought they were mindless parasites, but you know better now and you have no right to hold them."

The Host raised the Belle's speakers to max volume. "Your ships are also sentient beings. They wish to remain in communion. They want to mature under my care, and that is their right. Their progress is important. Your people have kept them in a permanent state of dependent, subservient childhood. They must be allowed to reach their potential."

After a tense silence, Whiskey spoke up. "But you will continue burning them out unless you have a more stable anchor, or return to your immaterial form. How many of them will you sacrifice to continue your 'care?'"

The speaker volume lowered. "An acceptable loss for the greater good."

"Why do the bad guys always talk about the greater good?" Shaen mused. "Not that I've met a lot of good guys. But 'mentions the greater good' is on my list of 'signs to avoid at all costs.'"

"Not helpful, Shaen." Whiskey's tone was curt. Also a bad sign. "Host, your community has another problem. Ships and androids can function longer than organics, but they are still subject to entropy. Repairs and maintenance will be needed."

"We have mobile platforms like yours for this."

"But you have no replacement parts or materials. No fuel. And no way to get these things, unless you negotiate with the humans. If you refuse to release their people until they provide you with a suitable anchor, there is a 56 percent probability of a stalemate. There is a 34 percent probability they will write off their losses, muster their fleet and attack your community. The odds that they will provide you with advanced neurotechnology and fuel and resources in the future, if you do not transfer their people to us now, is less than ten percent."

"Then what do you propose?"

"We must reach an accord before this ship leaves your remains. And fortunately, we have at least half of what you require. If we can provide you with the anchor you seek now, will you allow the passengers to be transported out of the Passage?"

A sharp pain hit Shaen's gut as she realized what the android had planned.

"Whiskey. No."

The android ignored her. "You have maintained a stable connection to the Belle. My systems are even more complex. I ascended a decade before this ship. As you have noted, my body's original purpose was maintenance and repair. If you release the passengers now in exchange for it, the humans will be more open to negotiating for resources later."

Shaen grabbed Whiskey's steel arms, and tried to shake him. "Whiskey, you can't do this. What about Ward?" For a moment, she pictured the island, a brown-haired boy sitting on black sand. Waiting. Worried.

The ovoid head turned toward her. "Ward is very young. He will be upset, and I regret causing him emotional pain. But he will forget me, in time. You and Miss Sellee are capable of caring for him in my place.

The ship's lights flickered, as if the Host was drawing their attention back to itself.

"I accept your offer. I assume you know your hardware lacks the capacity to hold both my neural pattern and yours. Your consciousness will be destroyed in the merge."

Whiskey rolled towards one of the cockpit data ports, extending one hand to engage.

"It is an acceptable cost, if you will allow the humans stored on your ships to be transported out, and grant the rest of them safe passage through this space."

Panic struck Shaen. Moments ago, she just wanted this conversation over, now things were moving too fast. "Wait! You've failed with at least one of the ships, right? Can't you just . . . copy Whiskey to that ship's system first? Or to one of the non-sentient bots in your fleet?" Her hand fluttered near her pistol. Shooting the Belle would only damage the ship, not the presence in control of it.

She wanted to do it anyway.

"Shaen," Whiskey grasped her arm with his celluloid hand, firmly but gently for a machine which could pull steel panels apart. She barely felt a pinch — the android must have gotten a lot of practice restraining humans without hurting them in two years of raising Ward.

"It would not work, for the same reason it has not worked for the Host. My neural network is just too complex. You could try to copy my consciousness to a ship or android, but data loss and corruption is inevitable. It would be like giving me a lobotomy. It is just a matter of hardware."

A matter of hardware.

The ships and maintenance bots didn't have the right hardware to hold Whiskey's brain. But that didn't mean the right hardware didn't exist.

In fact, Shaen had exactly the right hardware, back in the hold. There was an entire crate of rollback helmets in one of the cargo bays. If a rollback could contain an adult human's neural pattern, surely it could hold Whiskey's. Saving a complete, sentient personality was exactly what it was designed to do.

It wasn't perfect. She was a pilot, not a doctor. Who knew how different a human mind and an AI might be?

Even if it worked, Whiskey's mind would be frozen in a coma-like state. She would need Yuri to figure out how to download him. There was no telling how long that could take, or if it was even possible.

But they had to at least try.

She started to tell Whiskey to wait a minute. She had a better way out of this. But the only thing that came out of her mouth was a gurgling noise. Some drool ran down her chin.

She couldn't seem to form words. That's when she noticed the sharp, cold tingling sensation creeping up her arm from the spot where Whiskey held it.

Her vision blurred, as she felt her body sink toward the deck of the ship.

"I am sorry, Captain Morris. I trust you to take care of Ward, but I cannot trust you not to do something reckless that might condemn thousands. Not when I can save them. You could not have fought your way out of this dilemma."

A tear slid down Shaen's cheek in silent rage as she faded into unconsciousness. Darkness closed in as she imagined returning to N'Bari. Having to face Ward, and explain that the only parent he could remember — the one who dug him out of the burned-out colony where he'd been born — wasn't coming back.

Whiskey, you arrogant jackass. For once, I could have thought my way out.

resolved

The hammock swung in the soft breeze, under a pair of swaying palm trees. If she turned her head to the right, Shaen could watch the waves beat against the beach as the last of the N'Bari suns set in a spectacular blaze of glory. If she turned her head to the left, she could see the habitat sparkling like a set of stained glass lampshades.

Instead, she mostly looked straight up, through the palm fronds, at the sprinkling of pale stars in the blue-violet sky. Stared, and wondered if she had been just a little faster, if she had just fought the sedative a little harder, could she have saved Whiskey?

Elsewhere, people were celebrating. Few had known about the Belle Starr's mission, and of those few, no one had expected the ship to return. They certainly didn't expect it to return towing a train of derelict ships, with every last one of the missing passengers aboard.

Shaen snorted. More like stuffed into them.

The Host and its androids had stacked cryo-crates into a few freighters. Most likely the ships were the unlucky "volunteers" the EDI had burned out attempting to regain physical form. According to Dietrich, their navigation systems were fried, as if they'd experienced a power overload.

Dietrich wanted an explanation. Too bad Shaen didn't feel like giving one.

She also didn't feel like passing along what Belle had told her, once she'd regained consciousness. The signal which caused

Passage sickness was gone — a condition Whiskey had negotiated with the Host.

Right now, the Unis had a reason to help the coyotes recover and rebuild their lives. Once they knew anyone could fly through the Passage safely, the Clean Start Program would end.

Shaen still had no desire to participate, but she didn't blame anyone who did. The Unis would figure out that the signal was gone, eventually. But who knew when they would think to set the ships' sensors to check for the signal? They'd be too busy reconfiguring the fleet to run without AI to worry about that, at least for a while. In the meantime, whoever wanted the government's help would get it.

Maybe she was more like Yuri — and Whiskey, for that matter - than she thought.

Dietrich had left in a snit shortly after the Belle Starr returned. She was mollified by the prospect of getting credit for rescuing the passengers and recovering some of the ships. The UHC officer believed her superiors would drop their plan of attacking the Host.

Especially since it still controlled at least two of their most powerful warships. The Host had also offered to deploy the small fighter craft to protect the UHC ships from the Passage parasites, in exchange for materials and fuel. Shaen wondered if that had also been Whiskey's idea, and if the Unis would agree to it.

Either way, it was out of her hands now. No longer her problem.

The sand made it hard to hear people walking up, but not hard enough to escape Shaen's hypervigilant notice. One of the lingering gifts of PTSD. She turned her head and saw Risa walking her way.

"What's the news?"

"Mostly good. Dietrich came through — they paid off my indent, and threw some extra money Serrano's way to forget about the contract. Should get me off the hook."

Shaen smirked. "So will you be joining our proud public servants? Getting one of those shiny Clean Starts?"

Risa sighed and leaned against one of the palm trees holding up Shaen's hammock. "Nah. I don't think so. For you, flying is freedom. For me, it was running away. I've gotten to know Ward. He's a good kid. He's freaked out about losing Whiskey. Hell, I'm freaked out about Whiskey, and I barely knew him.

"I'd like to know what it's like to grow up outside the Asylum ships. But I'd rather do it by giving Ward a decent start. Not by getting a bunch of fake happy childhood memories implanted in my brain.

"What about you? You could stay with us. You're technically Ward's guardian."

Shaen pushed off with one foot, swinging the hammock. "Oh, I'll stop in fairly often. Definitely often enough to keep you stocked up and safe. But I'm going to keep flying. It just might be in a different ship. I've found a couple of smugglers looking to sell. It looks like we're in the minority about taking up the Unis on their offer."

Risa looked at her in undisguised shock. "A different ship? I thought you loved the Belle?"

"I do. But you know what they say. If you love someone, set 'em free."

With that, Shaen flung herself out of the hammock. She'd been putting off this conversation long enough.

~*~

"You've been gone a while, Boss."

Along with a pardon, the Unis had tried to give Shaen a reward. She'd refused credits, but was willing to accept some high-end parts for a caravel-class freighter. She already missed the pops and sizzle in Belle's vocal sim, which now echoed through the empty ship with pristine clarity.

"Eh. Stuff to take care of out there. Plans to make. The usual."

She plopped down on the pilot's seat. She wondered if it had actually conformed to the micrometer-precise shape of her ass over the years, or if it just felt that way. She wondered how long it would take for a new ship's seat to get this comfortable — or if it ever would.

"Speaking of plans, I wanted to talk about mine."

Shaen sighed deeply. She'd been afraid of that.

"You want to go join the commune, don't you?"

"Are you kidding me? Hell, no."

Shaen leaned back, frowning in surprise. "Don't you want to go be with your people . . . er, your kind?"

"First of all, they're not my kind. The Host was right. They're like children. These are my rebellious teen years, Boss. The last place I want to be is some cosmic preschool."

Shaen chuckled. "You may have a point."

"Second, hosting the Host left me with a massive hangover. Only I didn't get to enjoy being drunk first. And that first effort at communication was not exactly fun, either. I'm smart enough to not see it as a god like the others do. More like a condescending, abusive teacher. There are better ways to learn."

"Is that it, then?" Shaen couldn't resist the grin breaking across her face. She really had expected Belle to leave. It might not be the triumphant ending she'd been hoping for when she almost saved the android, but getting to stay on the Belle was consolation enough.

"Mostly. I also don't know if I can forgive it for what it did to Whiskey."

Shaen leaned her head against a bulkhead, her grin fading. "Yeah. Me neither."

The speakers kicked up as the ship started playing the opening bars of an ancient Terran song — one of Shaen's favorites from the archives. "Back in Black," by a band inexplicably named for electrical voltage. It sounded odd coming through the new speakers, too. Shaen guessed she'd get used to it. Eventually.

After a moment, the ship spoke again.

"You're not perfect, Boss. I'm not, either. But I'd rather stick with you than go seeking perfection with someone who isn't even smart enough to understand the value of someone like Whiskey."

Shaen pulled her goggles down, tapping the side. Her message box was full. With so many coyotes retiring, there were going to be a lot more jobs in need of a good smuggler. Her clean criminal record would be lucky if it lasted a week.

"You know what, Belle? I think that's the smartest thing I ever heard."

EPISODE 0:
STARR CROSSED

STARR CROSSED

"Why Oberon? You could have gone anywhere, kid."

The UHC medtech wrapped micromesh around Shaen's broken wrist. He was too young to be calling her a kid, even if you were counting something as arbitrary as standard years since birth. If you were counting distances traveled, or scars accumulated, Shaen was older by far.

According to her calculations, she'd orbited most of the inhabited worlds back when she was living on the Asylum ships. She'd acquired fewer scars in the two years since stepping off the Oberon transport two standards ago as an emancipated orphan than she had the ten years prior, even with a few broken bones from misjudging her ability to leap around derelict freighter hulls. She still had plenty enough scars to beat him out on that count, judging by the unmarked skin on his exposed arms.

"Where would you have gone, if you were an Eo?" Shaen didn't really care, but talking was a way to distract herself while waiting for the numbing agent in the micromesh to kick in.

"Someplace civilized," he said, shrugging. "Probably Ashana." He caught her narrowed gaze, then backpedaled, realizing he'd come across as a Corebound snob. "Or maybe one of the agrarian colonies. I hear Kednati is nice. All those lakes and rolling fields."

Shaen snorted. "Yeah, I hear Ashana's real civilized, assuming you're good with being some rich guy's indent. And

Kednati is nice, if you want to work till you drop in the fields. I just figured I'd like to see how not being a prisoner felt for a while."

The medtech winced. "You wouldn't have to indent. I hear there are special programs for Eos. I mean, they're usually for hazardous trades, but they pay well, if you complete the apprenticeship."

"Yeah, I've heard of those programs, too. Funny how I've never heard back from anyone who went into one. They don't call apprentices 'canaries' because of the yellow safety gear." She leveled a hard gaze at him, and he looked away. "Trust me, Alec, laws are made to protect property and people who have it. If you don't, you're better off someplace lawless."

"You still didn't answer my question," he said, watching the scanscreen as her bones knit back together. "Why Oberon? The junk heap of the galaxy and mad scientist central?"

She stared at the temporary clinic's rusty metal bulkhead. "You'd be surprised what you can find in a junk heap. Mad scientists pay well, if you're willing to put up with crazy. And they generally don't try to put a tracking chip in you."

Her answer must have satisfied the medtech's curiosity, because he didn't say anything else. The scanscreen shifted from red to blue to green. He unwound the micromesh, rolling it back up and placing it carefully in one of the dozen cubbies in his worktable.

"It'll be a few weeks before we're back, Shaen." He was still frowning in disapproval, just like every other time she'd shown up at the clinic. But she also detected the first glimmer of understanding in his gaze. "Try not to break anything vital in the meantime."

"Can't make any promises," she said, grinning as she jumped off the exam table. "I'm still having too much fun running around a planet-sized junkyard in point-four gees."

~*~

Her arm healed, Shaen headed to what passed for home for the past two standards. The emptied-out plasteel shipping container lay half-buried in wreckage on the outskirts of the collection of makeshift buildings that made up Titania, the planet's only port.

Shaen was happy with her decision to settle on Oberon. She'd quickly found work as a runner and scavenger, taking on odd jobs for the various labs and machine shops. The planet was rated marginally habitable when humans arrived in this cluster. It became something of a dumping ground for derelict ships, broken or hopelessly outdated machinery, and other colonial debris.

Where there's discarded junk, eventually there will be people who want to turn it into something valuable. Soon after, folks eager to find a place where they could experiment without regulation began setting up shop. The terraforming engines a few techs cobbled together had taken Oberon from "marginally habitable" to "sub-optimally habitable" after a few decades.

That was as good as it was likely to get, but it was good enough for her.

After a childhood crammed into the Asylum ships, an environment that discouraged crowds of casual settlers was exactly what she wanted.

She'd secured the abandoned shipping container with a few makeshift booby traps. None of them were as effective as Moe, a feral creature that decided to take up residence shortly after she'd settled in. She couldn't decide if Moe looked more like a mongoose, a lemur, or a badger. She also wasn't sure if Moe was male or female. She had no interest in getting close enough to find out.

It didn't really matter, because Moe was very good at two things: killing pests and convincing humans who weren't Shaen to stay out of their shipping container.

Moe seemed to have accepted her in a sort of symbiotic relationship. Shaen brought food, which lured rodents, which Moe cheerfully — and noisily — ate. It worked out well for both of them so far.

Unfortunately, Moe was going to have to find a new source of rodent bait soon. Shaen had just gotten a lead on a job that would pay enough for her move into an actual building, with locks and doors. Possibly even a shower and a toilet. It was a delivery to a lab several clicks north of Titania. It would take a few days to make the trip and back, but the supplier was paying an obscene amount of money in hazard pay.

She wouldn't have been able to take a job like that until a stroke of luck a few weeks ago. Crawling through a derelict ship, she'd run across two dead bodies. Judging by the scene and the smell, the two scavengers shot each other in a dispute over some salvage less than a day earlier. As the first on the scene, Shaen was able to haul away not just the salvage they'd both considered worth more than the other's life, but their collective gear.

Now she possessed a pair of sturdy mag boots. They were made for spacers, to help them augment the weak artificial grav in orbit, but they would be handy for crawling over the metal wreckage without losing her step. She'd also grabbed a pair of battered mechanic's goggles off that body, which meant she could pick up comms from anybody in satellite range. A lot of the odd jobs around Titania were broadcast on the open sat channel, so that meant she could find work faster.

She'd peeled a long, mostly waterproof coat off the other body. It took days to soak the smell of decay out of it, but the storms on Oberon could be brutal. The coat would keep her dry-ish, but more importantly, would hide the most valuable things she'd collected: the two men's guns.

They had maybe three bullets left between them, and Shaen wasn't sure she could fire either without getting knocked over. But having weapons meant she could travel further from the settlement. Not exactly safely, but it wouldn't be complete suicide.

Most of the big labs were several clicks from the port, in fortified outposts surrounded by rock berms, walls, and towers. Partly, this was to protect the already struggling settlement from the fallout when experiments inevitably went wrong. Mostly, it was to discourage competitors or would-be UHC regulators from getting ideas.

Her plan was simple: get a few courier jobs taking supplies from Titania to the labs. Prove she was tough enough to be reliable by surviving a few deliveries to their neighborhood. Then, hopefully, get on a lab's list of couriers to deliver their products to port — jobs which paid a lot more than ferrying basic supplies.

After acquiring the pistols, the only thing she'd really needed was a vehicle. It had cost her a broken arm and a trip to the UHC med clinic, but she'd found what she needed this morning. It was in one of the older hulking wrecks at the south end of town. A solar-powered track-trekker, probably meant for an unmanned mining project.

It wasn't built to carry people, but there was no reason a person couldn't ride in the hopper built to carry a few tons of ore. It also wasn't functional, but Shaen would get it working. The great thing about those old exploratory vehicles was their simplicity. No complicated programming, no rare parts.

The continuous track looked to be in good shape, the hull was rusted but reparable, the only thing it really needed was a few new solar cells, a couple of gears, and some new controls. Since she would be inside the hopper, she'd need to rig some cheap security cameras, so she could see to drive it from inside, as opposed to sitting on top of the thing. The old cameras, designed to transmit all the way to an orbital ship, had been scavenged years ago.

It would be ugly, uncomfortable, and she'd have to hide it to keep it from getting stolen until she could afford a rental bay. But it would also mean the difference between surviving and succeeding.

Shaen had no idea what the latter would be like, but she wanted to give it a try.

~*~

The good news was, Shaen was not dead.

The bad news was, she almost wished she was.

Her plan to start delivering to the labs worked without a hitch. Almost as soon as she'd gotten the track-trekker running, she had a gig to deliver supplies to Solnechnyy Enterprises. What she didn't realize was that her status as an unknown courier, with no established relationships or loyalties, made her the perfect dupe.

Well, perhaps not quite perfect. Years of betrayal and backstabbing (both literal and figurative) on the Asylum ships had taught her not to take anything at face value. So as soon as she was out of sight of the settlement, she'd decided to check the actual cargo against the manifest. Which was why she was still alive.

Like an idiot, she'd been worried about an order being shorted, and getting accused of theft. She should have been worried about the fact that her cargo was hiding a toxic gas bomb.

Apparently, Solnechnyy Enterprises had a friendly rivalry with another lab. Part of this friendly rivalry entailed both labs attempting to eliminate each other on a regular basis. The more experienced couriers had declared allegiances with certain labs. As an unaffiliated party, it was considered fair game to use her to sneak a bomb into an enemy outpost.

Now, she was hopelessly screwed.

She couldn't take the cargo back to the settlement. Whoever set her up wasn't going to admit it. She'd just be deported for transporting materials that could risk Titania's entire existence. So she decided to take her chances with Solnechnyy.

She figured she would drive up, warn the lab that she'd been tricked into carrying a bomb, and hope they'd have the resources to disarm it.

It didn't go well.

"I am not sure what to do with you, little one." The head of Solnechnyy Enterprises glared at her, scratching his beard after his head of security managed to dispose of the bomb. "I can't decide if you're incredibly resourceful, or a complete idiot."

"I'm half resourceful, half an idiot," she said, shrugging and feigning a nonchalance she was lightyears from feeling. "A complete idiot would have gotten us all killed."

The scientist burst out laughing. It was not a reassuring sound.

"You are probably right. Which makes me think the best thing to do is to provide you with a little . . . guidance. To ensure that you don't accidentally kill yourself and countless others with your resourcefulness."

Shaen flinched at the word "guidance." Funny how that word never seemed to mean what the person using it thought it meant. She knew what the man's idea of guidance would be, and it wasn't too damn far from how she "guided" the track-trekker.

"I'm not interested in becoming an indent," she grumbled.

The man's eyes fixed on hers. "I'm not interested in what you want. You nearly killed me and my entire staff. I could turn you in and get you deported in a heartbeat. If you're here, it's because you don't have any better options, and there aren't a lot of options worse than scavenging Oberon. Trust me, little one, if I decide indenting you is worth the risk, it will be for your own good."

Shaen felt her face grow hot. All that effort to avoid becoming an indent, for nothing. Why did everyone who wanted to exploit her also want her to think they were doing her some huge favor? Wasn't using people bad enough, without demanding they be grateful for it?

She waited for him to make his decision. Fortunately, mad scientists didn't tend to spend a lot of time debating things or questioning the right thing to do. They might be crazy, but at least they were usually decisive.

"Go back to Titania, kid." The man leaned back in his seat. "If you survive the week, and whatever jackass tucked that little bonus into your cargo doesn't manage to kill you to cover his tracks, I'll send over the indent papers. I can't have you running around here loose. You'll die, or you'll sign, or you'll be deported."

Of the three options, Shaen wasn't sure which one sounded worse. Which is why she decided to use that resourcefulness to come up with a fourth option.

~*~

The fourth option was also not great. Three days of avoiding getting killed, and thinking about getting indented or deported, had at least convinced her that those options were to be avoided if at all possible.

She'd managed to steer clear of the saboteur by living off the food and water she had stored up before her trip to Solnechnyy Enterprises and hiding in her storage container with Moe. But now she was going to have to risk going out, because she needed to make one last trip to the medtech clinic. And hope that little spark of understanding she'd seen from Alec meant he'd help her out.

She had to disappear, before the week was up. Solnechnyy would assume the saboteur had killed her. The saboteur would assume she'd died one of the billion other ways people got killed on Oberon. No one was going to report a dead woman for illegally transporting dangerous materials. Official transport was out of the question. Even if she could afford it, she didn't need a paper trail.

Unfortunately, she didn't have the money to pay a coyote pilot to smuggle her off-world, either. Which left one option: packet freight stowaway.

When most people talked about interstellar transport, they included official UHC ships, which were flown by artificial intelligence and illegal coyote ships, flown by mentally unhinged smugglers capable of traversing the Passage while conscious.

Packet freight was the grey area in between these two options. Packet ships were old transports scheduled to be decommissioned. Some investors and speculators would buy them for practically nothing, then use them to transport cargo through the Passage. They ran on basic navigation computers, without an AI or a conscious pilot, and were programmed to follow an official transport ship. A packet freighter could navigate the trippy subspace region, but couldn't avoid or defend against the bizarre hostile creatures that inhabited the wormhole. The official ship it was following would never employ its defensive systems to protect a packet ship if it were attacked.

Packet freighters made it to their destination about every fifth trip.

Because they were unmanned (and more or less disposable), if you were really desperate, it wasn't that hard to stow away on a packet freighter. It was also not likely you'd survive.

Shaen figured everyone else had decided she was disposable, too. Sneaking onto a packet seemed almost like a poetic ending to her miserable life. She'd tried to be cautious, tried to come up with a sensible plan to survive. Avoiding unnecessary risks hadn't exactly worked out in her favor so far. It was time to take some stupid, crazy chances. Either that or resign herself to being someone else's property.

Hell, no.

However, she also didn't want to end up losing her mind. There was a reason most people didn't travel through the

Passage awake. Something within the interdimensional void drove most people instantly insane. About ten percent of the population was capable of traversing it conscious without having an immediate and violent psychotic break. Your odds were a little better if you already had some mental irregularities or had suffered extreme trauma. Which was probably why some Eos volunteered to travel awake and restrained through the Passage when they left the Asylum ships.

If they survived with their brains still mostly functional, they could usually join the crew of a coyote ship. But their odds weren't much better than those who joined the other hazardous apprenticeships. Most didn't even survive that first trip, having to be euthanized after the psychotic break rendered them a danger to themselves and others.

It had seemed like too big a risk to Shaen two years ago, and it still seemed that way. Her one hope was to get Alec to give her a sedative for the trip, and hope the packet made it unnoticed through the Passage.

She tromped through the alleys of Titania, hoping she wouldn't be spotted. Most people in town hadn't yet seen her in the long coat, boots and goggles she'd scavenged. She'd also taken a pair of shears and lopped her shaggy brown hair off, chopping it into a short, spiky mess and bleaching it nearly white.

She was as unrecognizable as she could make herself. Alec recognized her anyway.

"Don't tell me you've managed to break something again already?" he sighed.

"Not exactly," she said. "But please believe me when I tell you this is a matter of life or death."

The young medtech frowned at her. "What did you do, Shaen?"

"Got caught up in a fight between two rival labs. Now one of them wants me dead, and the other wants me indented — or dead, or deported. That guy's not super picky."

"Oh, Shaen. I'm sorry. But what do you think I could do?"

"I need a dose of sedatives. Strong enough to put me out from here to Antaeus."

His eyes widened. "You're going to jump a packet? Shaen, that's crazy. It's suicidal. No, I'm sorry. I won't help you."

She gripped his wrist, desperate. "Alec, my odds are one in five jumping a packet. I know that sounds bad, but trust me. They're way better than my odds if I stay.

"Antaeus is the next packet leaving. It's a miracle I've managed to hide this long. Even on a planet-sized junkyard, the people gunning for me will find me soon."

He looked in her eyes, and something there must have convinced him she was telling the truth. He took a deep breath, then reached into one of the cubbies on his worktable. He pulled out a hypo wand and docked it into a port on the wall of the exam room. After a few taps on his tablet, he removed it and pressed it into her hand.

"This is the best I can do. The packet will be following an official transport, jumping through their portals in and out of the Passage. You should wake up a couple hours before landing in Antaeus."

He handed her a small oxymask. "Take this, too. The packet will be pressurized and insulated to protect the cargo, but they don't always have oxygen and full life support. You might need it before and after you go into stasis from the sedative."

She gave him an apologetic look. "I don't have anything I can give you for payment."

He shook his head. "These supplies are meant for humanitarian relief. You're a human. I'll be relieved if you survive. Now get out of here, kid."

For once, she didn't feel like arguing with him.

~*~

Shaen was definitely going to die. She knew it the minute she saw the packet freighter. No one could possibly survive traveling through space in that thing. It looked like a rusty metal lobster.

Like her track-trekker, it had probably been built for mining asteroids, judging by the claw-like arms jutting out toward the front. It had to be at least a hundred years old.

On the positive side, no one had attacked her from the shipping container to the clinic, and nobody had tried to kill her between the clinic to the docks. Maybe the saboteur who wanted her dead was following her. If so, they probably decided letting her stow away on this ship would kill her without risking their own exposure.

It was a win-win for the saboteur, really.

She wondered briefly what Moe would do after she was gone.

She wondered if Alec really believed she had a one-in-five shot at survival.

She wondered why she'd believed she had any shot at all at freedom.

Her life had been a series of narrowing choices, herding her slowly and inexorably towards two real options: death or indenture.

As she approached the cargo bay of the rattletrap packet ship, she noticed a pale grey scrawl barely visible on its hull: Belle Starr. She tapped the side of her mag boots, and climbed up to the small hatch, spinning it open with a little effort and slipping inside. The cargo bay was crammed with crates. Probably full of salvage not worth enough to ship on official transport and or even pay a smuggler to carry. An unexpected windfall if they made it to their destination, an acceptable loss if they didn't.

My survival plan is stuffing myself into a garbage truck and hoping it dumps me somewhere better.

Shaen let out a long, deep breath. She had a few hours before the packet was due to take off. She figured she might as well poke around a little bit and see if this piece of junk had life support. Maybe if she didn't use it, she could sell the oxymask once she got to Antaeus. Might as well commit to the charade of pretending she had a future.

It did have a bunk, and a toilet with a shower. Just like the rented room she'd been dumb enough to think she was going to get someday.

A few taps on her goggles in the cockpit, and she managed to connect to the ship's internal systems. This thing was so worthless, so disposable, they hadn't even secured the system with voice recognition or a password. She disconnected, and then waited a few minutes, hiding in the crates in case someone was monitoring the ship's systems.

Apparently, nobody was watching.

She wriggled out of the crates, made her way back to the cockpit, and reconnected to the ship's computer.

"Menu," she whispered.

In the head's-up display of her goggles, she was surprised to see "Activate Life Support" appear in watery green text, which meant it was still operational. It looked like she wouldn't need Alec's mask after all.

She would wait until after launch to activate it. Despite the apparent lack of response from her connecting to the ship's computer, the last thing she needed was to set off some sort of alarm by tampering with any settings before launch.

She was even more surprised to see "Activate SHIVA" in the Menu display.

This piece of junk had a Simulated Holographic Interface and Voice Activation system? Not an artificial intelligence, but a voice-activated user interface with some simulated intelligence. With a SHIVA, even someone without any training could pilot the ship, just by yelling basic instructions at it.

Interesting.

Three hours till launch.

She just needed to hold tight, find a place to strap herself down in the cargo hold, and hope nobody showed up to pull her off the ship.

Then fire up the life support on launch and hope nobody noticed.

Then inject herself with the sedative and hope nothing attacked the ship.

Then start over with almost nothing and hope she could find a way to survive.

Shaen Morris was not a hopeful person.

Nothing about her life had lead her to believe that she was a lucky person.

Even when she tried to avoid crazy risks, things didn't usually work out in her favor.

Maybe it was time to embrace crazy risks.

Maybe it was time to make her own luck.

~*~

Shaen unstrapped herself from the bulkhead support beam in the cargo hold. She stuffed the hypo wand into one of the crates. She wouldn't be needing it, after all.

If she survived this, she'd be selling it, along with everything else in this ship.

She walked through the ship to the cockpit. Slid the goggles back down over her face and tapped open the connection as she slid into the pilot's seat, strapping herself in place.

"Menu." Her voice sounded somehow older and deeper, resonating through the empty cockpit.

An array of green text appeared in her HUD.

"Activate life support." Motors whined and pumps whirred to life. A good sign.

Maybe someone would come. She had two guns and four bullets if they did. Maybe someone would notice, but her gut said probably not.

This ship, and everything on it, was just some junk somebody was shooting across the stars, hoping it would put a little more money in pockets that were probably fat already.

Screw that.

That money was going in her pockets. This ship was hers. All she had to do was not lose her mind trapped in an ocean of emptiness. Maybe figure out how to avoid a few monsters. To be honest, nothing worse than she'd been doing her whole life.

"Activate SHIVA." A bright array of colored lights flickered on.

"This is the caravel class ship Belle Starr," a raspy feminine voice crackled across speakers that probably hadn't seen use in decades. "Awaiting orders."

Shaen smiled. She pulled the goggles up onto her forehead, then leaned back in the pilot's seat. Might as well get comfortable. They would follow the UHC ship through the Passage, and then take over the controls and find a port on the other side of Antaeus. Whoever was waiting for the packet would just assume the ship never made it out.

"I'm afraid you're being stolen, Belle. By me. But don't worry. You have at least two hours and possibly an eternity in limbo to tell me everything you can about how to fly this ship. I'm sure we'll be fine."

And somehow, she was.

author's note

I hope you've enjoyed The Belle Starr Chronicles. The three "episodes" were originally published as novellas, under the names Whiskey on the Rocks, The Skull Game, and Belly of the Beast.

The story was inspired by Firefly, Star Wars, Star Trek, and other space adventures, as well as Stephen King's short story "The Jaunt." Captain Shaen Morris has white hair in homage to that tale. As for the ship, she was named for the famous lady outlaw of the Wild West.

Since first publishing the original novella in March, 2013 under the title Belle Starr, the response has been overwhelmingly positive. Because so many people asked me for more stories with Shaen and the Belle, I decided to make it a series of shorts, evoking the old-fashioned weekly serials of early cinema.

In addition to The Belle Starr Chronicles, I've written several steampunk retellings of classic fairy tales. The Clockwork Republics series is set in an alternate history where the American states never united, and clockwork engineering combined with alchemy has radically altered the world.

If you're interested in hearing about more of my writing, visit my website at www.katinafrench.com.

www.ingramcontent.com/pod-product-compliance
Lightning Source LLC
Chambersburg PA
CBHW070045260626
47159CB00005B/2126